"Do I make you nervous?" Rusty asked. There was a teasing quality to his velvet baritone, a honeyed Louisiana drawl that sent shivers down Kevyn's spine.

"Yes. . . ." The word was soft, but hung heavy and expectant in the air.

"Are you afraid of me?" Rusty asked.

"Not of you." The feeling of danger skidded through her veins.

He inhaled deeply. "You feel it too? It's why I came back." His strong fingers hovered near her face, brushing a strand of silver-streaked hair back. "It scares the heck out of me, but I can't leave it alone."

Her skin tingled where his fingertip had touched it. She felt the warmth of his gaze like a physical caress, touching her body and testing the depths of passion inside it. She was as trapped by his power as if his hands held her in their grasp.

"What is it?" he demanded softly. "Tell me what we're afraid of."

"We're too different from each other. We're going to get hurt."

"Maybe. But I've learned to look beyond the fear and pain, if I think the end result will be worth it. Tell me, Kevyn, is it worth the risk?" He lowered his lips to hers, and no amount of willpower or even fear could stop her hungry surrender. . . .

WHAT ARE *LOVESWEPT* ROMANCES?

They are stories of true romance and touching emotion. We believe those two very important ingredients are constants in our highly sensual and very believable stories in the *LOVESWEPT* line. Our goal is to give you, the reader, stories of consistently high quality that may sometimes make you laugh, sometimes make you cry, but are always fresh and creative and contain many delightful surprises within their pages.

Most romance fans read an enormous number of books. Those they truly love, they keep. Others may be traded with friends and soon forgotten. We hope that each *LOVESWEPT* romance will be a treasure—a "keeper." We will always try to publish

LOVE STORIES YOU'LL NEVER FORGET
BY AUTHORS YOU'LL ALWAYS REMEMBER

The Editors

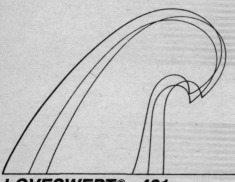

LOVESWEPT® • 421

Patricia Burroughs
Some Enchanted
Season

 BANTAM BOOKS
NEW YORK • TORONTO • LONDON • SYDNEY • AUCKLAND

To Patricia Boyce,
whose endurance, laughter, and soaring spirit
are an inspiration.

To Ruth Cohen, Literary Agent,
who believed.

To Nancy Gramm, sister Pleiad,
may your star always shine.

SOME ENCHANTED SEASON

A Bantam Book / September 1990

If you would be interested in receiving protective vinyl
covers for your Loveswept books, please write to this
address for information:

Loveswept
Bantam Books
P. O. Box 985
Hicksville, NY 11802

ISBN 0-553-44052-7

Published simultaneously in the United States and Canada

PRINTED IN THE UNITED STATES OF AMERICA

OPM   0 9 8 7 6 5 4 3 2 1

One

"Fools." Kevyn Llewellyn sighed and longed for a cup of steaming lemon water and her own warm bed. "They must be fools."

Shivering at the edge of misty Cross Lake, she pivoted slowly and forced her attention to her immediate need—a god.

She slid her gaze from the serene lake to the bustling, swarming scene of activity before her. To get to the water's edge, she had weaved through a throng of over six hundred athletes from across the nation, all preparing to begin the first leg of the fifty-one kilometer Shreveport Triathlon. Bemused, she considered the athletes' upcoming endeavor: swimming one kilometer through water that was still chilly from the previous evening's thunderstorm; biking forty kilometers on winding asphalt roads; and then completing the circuit with a ten-kilometer run that was intensified by the hilly terrain and humid, blistering Louisiana August heat. "Fools," she repeated, and wondered what she was for being there among them.

As she worked her way along the pine- and cypress-lined banks toward the parking area, she dodged the out-flung arms and avoided the outstretched legs of the triathletes as they warmed up.

"Crazy jocks," she muttered, folding her arms across her chest for warmth. Her black cotton middy dress had lost its crispness in the damp haze.

"Auntie!" a resonant voice rang out.

It was about time, she thought, casting a glance toward the road, where a large van with the radio call sign KPOP scrawled across its side in orange and green letters was parked. Sure enough, Kevyn saw her nephew Atticus darting through the athletes, oblivious to their glares.

"Wait up!" His hair bounced in glossy waves as he crossed the uneven ground in loping bounds. He came to a halt beside her, panting from the exertion. She glared up at mischievous eyes the same deep teal color as hers, a nose tip-tilted only slightly less, and the same silver-streaked hair at the temples that was a Llewellyn family trademark. "Sorry," Atticus said. "I've been tied up with details. These remotes are a dog to pull together. I've got a couple of minutes before air time, though. So, how's it going? Enjoying the view, Auntie dear?"

Kevyn followed his gaze to a burly athlete, who eyed her speculatively before stripping off his muscle shirt, obviously for her benefit. Quickly, she grabbed Atticus's arm and tugged him along with her toward a spot at the fringe of the activity.

Atticus grinned. "What's the hurry?"

"In the first place, how many times do I have to tell you? Don't call me 'Auntie.' It sounds ridiculous, and you know it. After all, you're six inches taller than I am, not to mention two years older."

"But you are my aunt, Kevvie. Blood kin, much as you might wish to disown me." He dropped an arm around her shoulders as they moved on. "It *is* an unusual situation, you must admit."

"Not as unusual as you think," Kevyn grumbled. "You make it seem so bizarre, the way you always call attention to us—like jogging through hundreds of people shouting 'Auntie' when a simple 'hey, you' would do."

"But it's so much fun," he insisted.

"For you, maybe, but not for me. I don't appreciate being introduced as your old maid aunt either. Save your attention-getting devices for your show. I have enough trouble dealing with the real you, much less your alter ego." With studied disdain, she removed his arm from her shoulder. "I don't know why I put up with your nonsense. I've known fourteen-year-olds who were more mature than you."

"You haven't answered me. Have you found a victim—I mean, a man you like?"

"Atticus, it isn't a matter of what *I* like. It's a matter of what Fantasy Books wants." She kicked a tuft of tall grass. "This whole project is giving me ulcers," she grumbled. "If I didn't need the money so badly . . ." Her voice drifted away. The problem was, she did need the money. "I've just never had this much trouble finding a model before, that's all."

"It seems I remember you saying the artwork for this book cover would be a snap."

"I must have looked at a thousand pictures. All 'pretty boys.' You know the type: sultry and spoiled, sullen and pouty, and perfect for lounging poolside on the pages of *GQ*. But nothing even remotely physical enough for"—she paused, then lowered her voice dramatically—"*Darius: Warrior God of the Gray Planet.*" Her laughter sounded a bit strained, even to her own ears.

"Sounds like a thirties radio show, to me."

"You should know."

"You can't tell me you aren't interested in all the beefcake that's strutting around here," Atticus remarked with a sly gleam in his eyes.

She wrinkled her nose in distaste and faced the crowd again. "I don't know why I let you talk me into coming to this ridiculous triathlon. I should have stayed in bed. Look at them," she insisted. "Not an ounce of brain in the lot of them."

"Now, Kevyn. We mustn't judge, eh? Besides, isn't brawn what you need?"

"No. That's exactly the point. He's muscular, of course, but not brawny. He's intelligent and noble and valiant and . . ." She tucked a strand of hair behind her ear. "My deadline's in three weeks, and I'm desperate. I've got to find someone."

"Well, I'm afraid you're going to have to do your

own hunk-hunting. The blondes I have in mind are a bit curvier, if you get my drift." Atticus straightened her hat and tweaked her lightly on the nose. When she tried to retaliate with a halfhearted swat, he darted away, sing-songing, "So long, Auntie dear . . ."

Kevyn watched him bound off toward the remote transmission van where he'd be broadcasting the morning's activities. She attempted to stifle her smile, with little success. They were close, though their relationship was certainly not that of an aunt and nephew. He was more like a brother, or a friend . . . and quite often, an albatross.

An announcement over the public-address system warned the athletes that they had five minutes before the race started. To gain a better vantage point, Kevyn moved to the crest of a low hill, pulled an old, tattered quilt from her straw carryall, and spread it on the damp grass. After producing a sketch pad, a case of artists' pencils, and a camera, she dropped to the ground.

Her sharpened pencil poised, she perused the area, seeking inspiration. Her gaze drifted until it settled on a masculine pair of legs walking toward her. Lazily, her gaze slid upward, then locked on lean, muscled thighs moving in a sleek, lynxlike rhythm. . . .

Powerful legs—certainly capable of striding masterfully across the heavy atmosphered terrain of Euripides, the Gray Planet . . .

Her interest heightened, she dragged her eyes up, over the navy-blue competition swimsuit that molded every bulge. She memorized the smooth flat planes of stomach, the wide expanse of chest, and broad shoulders . . .

This body was made for more than lounging poolside in a swimsuit ad. This body belonged to a warrior who moved with all the grace of a god— Darius.

He strode past before she had recorded a single, exquisite detail. Springing to her feet, she allowed the pencil and pad to fall unheeded to the rumpled quilt. She stifled a familiar pang of frustration as she strained to see the number emblazoned on the man's bright yellow swimcap, but could only make out two rounded digits as he melted into the crowd of triathletes.

"I never got a good look at his face," she grumbled, then chuckled. She'd certainly gotten a terrific view of everything else.

Suddenly, the crack of the starter's pistol signaled the beginning of the race, and the stampede began. Within seconds the racers had turned the placid lake into a churning, splashing cauldron of activity. Peering across the water, she was appalled at the number of competitors wearing yellow swim caps, evidently official triathlon issue. How was she ever going to find Darius in that crowd?

Twenty minutes later the leaders had completed the roughly circular route marked by buoys and row-boats filled with safety personnel. Kevyn walked with the other spectators to the man-made beach, where the swimmers had entered the water and would now emerge. Standing behind the barricade, she watched them come out of the lake, first in a trickle, then in larger groups. Five minutes passed, then ten and fifteen, without any sign of Darius.

Finally she spotted a lone swimmer drawing near the shore. What he lacked in speed, he obviously made up for in endurance. The rolling action of his shoulders as the muscles moved beneath the surface of his skin, his hands slicing cleanly into the choppy water—these were images that captivated her imagination. Her fingers tingled and itched to sketch his musculature. Darius. He had to be the one.

He rose from the lake, water streaming down his body in shimmering rivulets, tracing every contour. His head fell forward as his golden chest heaved. He stretched his neck, then rolled his head from side to side before rotating his shoulders.

Close enough to touch him, Kevyn remained spell-bound as he lifted his face toward the sun. His high cheekbones and the hollows beneath them, the hard, lean angles of his face, all combined to lend him a foreign look. European? Nordic? Slavic? she wondered.

A tremor of excitement shot through her body. Her search was over. This *was* Darius. Her mind swirled with visions, startlingly clear now that her indecision was behind her. She visualized her painting: Darius standing triumphant, proud, arrogant, against a rich Prussian blue sky, his waist-long platinum hair and golden body bathed in silver moonlight.

Then he abruptly tugged the swim cap from his head, flung it to the ground, and started toward the changing tents. His hair wasn't blond—it was red.

It fell down his neck in damp, unruly auburn waves, the still-dry crown blazing with glints of gold and cinnamon, reflecting fiery touches of sunlight.

Kevyn's breath escaped in a low hiss, her lips parted. Red hair. The man had red hair. She knew a moment's panic as she continued to stare until he disappeared through the open tent flaps. Then, she knelt down and reached under the barricade to retrieve his swim cap. She wiped away a smear of mud. His number glared back at her.

Wadding the cap into a ball, she lifted her chin. All right. So the guy had red hair. Why should that bother her so much? He was still perfect, if she used a little artistic license. She strode toward a woman who clasped a clipboard against her bony chest.

"Excuse me." Kevyn smiled and pointed at the clipboard. "Is that a list of competitors?"

"Yes, it is." The woman angled a weathered face toward her. "This is the official roster."

"One of the athletes lost his swim cap, and I'd like to return it to him. Could you tell me his name, please?"

The woman hesitated, then held out the clipboard. "I doubt if he'll want it back, but you can look."

"Oh . . ." Kevyn stared at the clipboard as she

clutched the damp, mud-spattered swim cap. "You'd better look for me. My hands are dirty."

The woman shrugged and glanced at the number on the swim cap, then flipped past the top sheet. She ran a finger down the second page. "Here it is, number 86. Oh, dear . . . how do you pronounce this?"

Again she held the clipboard out for Kevyn's perusal, but Kevyn shook her head.

"Sergay? Sergee?" the woman asked. "That's some kind of Russian name, isn't it?"

"Yes, that's definitely Russian," Kevyn agreed. "I don't know how to pronounce it either." No wonder he had such a distinctively European look to him, she thought.

"Sergei Rivers. That's an unusual name," the woman mused. "It sounds kind of familiar, but I can't quite place it."

Rivers? Kevyn frowned. She thanked the woman and started up the slope. With Atticus tied up for the entire day, it was up to her to locate the mysterious warrior-god.

Long hours dragged by before she found him again. She sat in her parked Volkswagen bug convertible on the side of the road where the last portion of the race was taking place. She brushed an annoying strand of silver-streaked hair from her eyes and lifted her hair off her neck. Fighting off thirst, gnats, and a ferocious headache, she was at the point of giving up.

Then he rounded a curve and came limping down the road toward her. One of his legs was badly scraped, yet he ran on. "Fool," she muttered. But all she could do was wait. He would pass her again on his return trip from the turnaround checkpoint up the road.

The runners who passed looked progressively worse, more winded, more heated, more exhausted. Kevyn swatted a fly away from her face and glanced up the road. Sergei Rivers should have been back by now, she realized.

She couldn't forget how exhausted he had looked when he'd limped past. She twined her fingers in her hair and leaned forward on the steering wheel. The thought of that magnificent body collapsing with heatstroke set her nerves on edge.

Finally, she couldn't take it any longer. She glanced at her watch and wiped her arm across her brow. Grabbing her bag, she jumped out of the car and started after him. She hadn't spent hours waiting for the guy to have him pass out and get carted away before she could use him.

Then she saw him.

He struggled, stumbling along, thrusting one foot in front of the other, his eyes fixed doggedly on the road.

Without pausing to think, Kevyn scurried toward him, her hair tumbling around her shoulders, her wide-brimmed hat bouncing on her back. "Excuse me, er . . . Ser-gay, or Ser-gee—oh, how *do* you pronounce your name?"

His head snapped toward her. For a moment, his eyes remained unfocused. Then they fixed on hers, his gaze hard and piercing. "Who . . . are you?" His hoarse voice sent shivers skidding down her spine.

"Are you all right?" she demanded.

He said nothing, but kept trudging along, determination etched on his flushed, drawn features.

Kevyn jogged hesitantly beside him, her mind racing. What was she supposed to do? "You look like you're in trouble," she began. "Are you sure you're okay?"

His face was beaded with sweat, his hair plastered to his brow, his eyes dazed as he squinted against the glare of the midday sun. It seemed to take all of his energy simply to move, let alone answer.

"You've got to stop," she panted. "Your leg looks awful, and you're going to have a stroke if you don't cool off!"

"Buzz off, lady," he choked out without turning

his attention from the road. "I'm fine . . . I'm doin' just fine," he mouthed, as if talking to himself.

"That's ridiculous. You certainly are not fine. Just look at you. Why—" With a softer voice, she tried a different tactic. "Why don't you stop and rest?"

"I'm . . . fine. . . ." He swung out his arm as if to show her, his hand brushing against her bare forearm.

"Please." Kevyn rubbed the spot where his touch had scorched her. "I can't afford for you to hurt yourself."

He didn't respond.

Her throat stung, and her head pounded with each step. As they rounded another curve, Kevyn saw her yellow Volkswagen beckoning invitingly.

Suddenly, the man's foot caught in a pothole, and he crashed to the asphalt.

Kevyn dropped to her knees, ignoring the gravel biting into them, and reached out. "Oh, gracious! Are you hurt?" He rolled to his side and clutched his leg. She gasped at the sight of blood running through his fingers. "Look what you've done. Your leg!" She dug frantically in her bag for tissues.

He lay there as she dabbed the gash, then shook his head as if to clear it. "Who are you?" he asked weakly.

"My name's Kevyn." She offered her hand. "Here, let me help you up." Between her pulling and his will-power, she managed to stand him upright, though he leaned heavily on her shoulders for a moment before he could attempt to stand alone. He wiped a hand across his brow, then down the side of his face, a smear of blood tracing its path. Turning a pained gaze toward her, he tried to straighten. "I'm not . . . quitting."

Kevyn attempted to hide her dismay. This man wasn't determined—he was obsessed. Her own shoulders slumping, she watched as he tried to take off, and stumbled. Only by ducking quickly under his arm did she manage to keep him from crashing to the pavement again.

"Gotta finish . . ." he muttered. ". . . almost there . . . aren't I?"

"No. You've got over half a mile to go."

"Not far . . ." He lurched forward.

She tried to hang back, but his momentum propelled her forward.

"Help me. . . . I've . . . gotta . . . finish. . . ."

"Lord, I'm as big a fool as you are," she said as she stumbled beside him. She desperately scanned the road for more potholes. As they half-ran, half-staggered along, she watched the hypnotic pattern of their feet moving in unison. "You're going to owe me, I hope you realize that."

She drew him near her car, and visions of home and icy pink lemonade danced in her aching head.

"Fifty-one kilometers . . ." he muttered under his breath. "Then . . . I'll win . . ."

Kevyn filled with compassion. "I hate to break this to you, but the man who won this race finished two and a half hours ago."

"I'll win the . . . the bet. Skipper . . ."

Kevyn stopped dead in her tracks, and he almost fell on his face again. "What did you say?"

His eyes clouded as they tried to focus on her. "Why—why'd we stop? We're almost there."

"A bet? Are you crazy?" Her flushed face grew redder. "You're about to pass out, and I'm practically carrying you, and it's just so you can win a lousy *bet*?"

"Look, babe." He lurched away from her. "Forget it. I don't need you." He started to move forward, but his injured leg gave out again.

Yet again, Kevyn held him up, though anger surged through her.

"Of all the asinine, pigheaded things I've ever heard," she sputtered, lugging him toward the car, her fury growing with each pained step. "I'm about to keel over, my head is splitting open"—She propped him against the car, and he attempted to brace himself on the too-low side of the open convertible with trembling arms. "You look like you could just about *die* at any moment—and you want to keep going to win a *bet*?"

"It's important. You don't understand—"

"You're darn right, I don't. You're killing yourself to win a bet, and you expect me to go down with you? Buddy, I'm going to save you in spite of yourself." With that, she shoved him, and he landed in the backseat with a loud grunt, which dwindled into a moan.

Kevyn jumped into the driver's seat and slammed the door. As the car roared to life, he tried to raise himself up. "Just a damned minute—"

Glancing over her shoulder, she threatened, "You're not going to end up in a hospital recuperating from your lunacy when I need you now." The car jerked forward, and he fell back, his head hitting the door with a dull thud.

What was she supposed to do now? She sent a desperate prayer to the heavens—grateful to the powers that be for delivering this perfect warrior-god into her grasp, yet frantic for new inspiration as to how to handle him. Shifting gears, she made a sharp U-turn and roared away, leaving a spray of gravel in her wake.

Two

"Water . . ." The word ripped from Rusty's throat in a dry gasp. "My legs, my stomach . . ." His voice sounded like a hollow echo in his throbbing head. "Lord, I'm dying. . . ." Someone was grinding steel cleats into his calves, grinding and twisting red-hot blades deep into the muscles of his legs and his stomach. His throat was parched sandpaper, his mouth filled with sawdust. He tried to swallow.

A hand touched his forehead. "Your temperature's down," a woman's voice said as he blinked, straining to focus. Before he could respond, she pulled her hand away.

He opened his mouth to speak and felt something cool and hard press against his lower lip.

"Here, drink this."

He stretched toward the glass and gulped at the trickle of water. His thirst wiped out all thoughts and questions. "More," he begged.

"Only a half an ounce for now," the voice said anxiously, withdrawing the glass. "Not too fast. How do you feel?"

"How do you think I feel?" he demanded through cracked, stinging lips. "I'm dying. Turn on the damn whirlpool and—and—for Pete's sake, turn up the heat and—and where's Ernie?"

"There isn't a whirlpool," the woman answered as she sponged his face. The ensuing chills alternately refreshed and infuriated him. Then, incredibly soft fingertips spread something moist and creamy and heavenly across his lips. "This aloe vera cream should help." She pulled her fingers away an instant before he succumbed to the ridiculous notion of sucking them into his mouth.

Rusty squinted, straining to focus on what seemed to be a stark image in black and white—a white face, with features his burning eyes couldn't recognize, and black hair, framing the face in stark midnight waves. A shiver of unease rippled through him, and again, he groaned at the pain.

"Who are you?" This was one time when, if someone with an ingratiating smile hovered over him and offered a hypodermic of novocaine, he'd be tempted to accept. He felt himself sinking lower into the pain . . . into cool, refreshing water. "Water," he demanded weakly. His large hand groped, then fell limply beside him.

"You have to drink it slowly."

He stared through the haziness and began to distinguish features . . . a raven-haired widow's peak, eyes of a smoky blue. . . . She turned away from him and receded into the periphery of his vision, leaving him oddly disturbed, dissatisfied.

The sound of running water tantalized him. She was filling a tiny glass at a sink. . . . An old-fashioned pedestal sink. . . . With a great effort, he moved his head. He wasn't at the rehab center. He was in a bathroom. He was in a bath . . . tub. A bathtub. He shook his head. "Wait a damn minute. Where am I?"

She appeared before him again with the glass. He gulped the water down. Before she could pull it away, he snatched the glass out of her hand and clumsily dipped it into the bath water. He quickly tossed the water down his throat, once, twice, three times.

"Stop it!" Cold water splashed over his head. He dropped the glass and she whisked it from the floor and out of his sight. "You're going to make yourself sick."

"I don't care," he said through clenched teeth. He

reached for his thighs and squeezed and kneaded, gasping as pain and relief battled for prominence in the much-abused muscles. "Lord, I'm cramping."

"I know . . . I know. . . ." she soothed. "Just be patient. . . ."

Again, he strained to focus his vision, and finally her features crystallized, none so telling, so incriminating as the odd threads of silver streaking her inky black hair. He strained to remember. He'd seen her before.

The fog cleared.

"You!" He sat up abruptly. "You—you made me lose my bet!"

"Now, sit back down before you swoon again," she scolded, and gave his shoulder a light shove. He fell back into the tub, splashing a wave of water over the edge.

"Where the hell am I?"

"Thank goodness. I believe Miss Lucy was right. All you need is a little more time, a little more water, and you'll be good as new."

"Who are you?" he demanded desperately.

"Shhh . . . just relax."

Dammit, that was all he seemed capable of doing. He drifted back into the fog without fighting. After he regained his strength, he'd figure out this damned mess.

Squatting by his side, Kevyn mopped his face with the sponge, mentally noting the straight nose and high cheekbones, facial contours that blended so strangely to produce such masculine beauty. For he was beautiful, in a virile way. She held the sponge in her hand, ignoring the water that ran down her arm and dripped from her elbow onto the floor as she stared at him. He appeared so large and real and overpowering, now that she had him up to his neck in tepid water in her tub.

Heart pounding with relief, she assumed a cross-legged pose on the closed toilet, her sketch pad and drawing pencil in hand. Finally reassured that he was in no immediate danger—that she hadn't made the most foolish and possibly imprudent decision of her life to save her contract—she sketched quickly. This was one sitting she'd better complete in a hurry, she knew, for beneath the surface of his exhaustion the man emanated the tension of a caged animal.

A very well-developed animal, at that. She snorted with disdain. His musculature was the product of hours, days, *years* in a gym. And if it seemed a trifle ungrateful to judge the vanity of the male who was providing her with the money she so desperately needed, well, she'd be grateful with her wallet.

The soft-leaded pencil flew across the page as she detailed his facial features. He began to stir, but was obviously not fully back in the real world. Yet, after a few minutes, Kevyn saw a discernible change in her warrior-god. His head seemed to clear, and this time when he braced his hands on the side of the tub and raised up, it was a controlled movement.

His damp auburn eyebrows lowered into a menacing glare. "What the hell is going on here?"

Kevyn tossed the pad aside and stood up. "Considering all I've done for you, I'd appreciate it if you'd stop cursing at me."

"Considering all you've done *to* me, I oughta do a lot more than cuss!" He pushed a wet shock of hair off his forehead and grabbed the sides of the tub as if to stand. Suddenly, the expression on his face changed dramatically, and his gaze lowered to his body. "Where the hell are my clothes?"

A small towel covered his lower torso under the water, though each swirling current threatened to dislodge it, and there was nothing under the towel except for—himself.

"We had to remove anything constricting. Don't worry," Kevyn reassured him. "I didn't undress you. Miss Lucy did."

"What?" He clutched at himself in an instinctively

protective gesture, his flushed face blanching. "Who in the hell is Miss Lucy?"

"Really, Mr. Rivers. You're cursing again." She frowned as she reached for her sketch pad and tossed him a towel.

"What's that you've got? You—you were—you were drawing me, weren't you?" he stammered.

"Your clothes are on the windowsill. I'm sure you can manage by yourself." Kevyn clicked shut the door and clutched her sketch pad tightly against her body. She needed more time, more sketches, not to mention his signature on a release form. Somehow, things weren't going as smoothly as she'd hoped. She'd banked on his gratitude.

Instead, she had a surly jock in need of a good soaping down.

Oh, well. She shrugged and felt a smile tugging at the corners of her lips. She'd give him a minute to cool off. He'd come around.

Rusty stared at the closed door with its faded turquoise paint peeling from large hinges, at the glass doorknob and the large keyhole below it, and felt a surge of panic. What if she locked him in, held him captive? He pulled shakily to his feet, glanced down at his body, and realized that one question superseded all others.

"Who in the hell is Miss Lucy?" Rusty thundered again, but received no reply from beyond the door. His fingers dug into the thick terry towel she had given him. Black? Whoever heard of black towels?

He began rubbing himself dry, wincing when the towel brushed over the raw scrape on his leg. He had to get out of this place. The room revolved a half-rotation, but he gritted his teeth and grabbed his running shorts. That woman was more than strange, she was spooky. That silver-streaked hair was bizarre, and those slanting eyes seemed to dissect him at will.

Spooky and bizarre and beautiful. Yes, downright

beautiful. But he'd be damned if he was going to let that fact interfere with finding the nearest exit.

Tugging his gray satin shorts over his hips, he attempted an instant replay of the events that had landed him here—wherever "here" was. He couldn't remember anything out of the ordinary. That is, until *she'd* entered the picture. The way she kept looking at him sent chills down his spine. He was used to being admired, even ogled, but something about the way this woman stared left him feeling . . . endangered.

He braced his hands on the sink and stared into the mirror, not liking what he saw there—his own haggard reflection. He had to leave before anyone besides Skipper discovered what an idiot stunt he'd pulled.

He yanked open the door and stepped into the dark hallway. She stood there, waiting, those strange, slanting eyes seeming to glow. "Where are my shoes?" he demanded.

"Oh, those." She stepped out of the shadows. "I threw them out the window. Your socks too. They stank something awful."

"Those are expensive running shoes, lady. I have prescription orthotics in those shoes!"

"Then the airing out will do them good. Come along with me, and I'll see if I can find you something to drink. Miss Lucy says you need plenty of fluids, but only a few sips at a time."

"Who is Miss Lucy?" he asked again.

"She lives downstairs. She's a sweet little old lady. A retired nurse. That's why she knew what to do for you when—" A grinding noise whirred from behind a square door in the wall. "I'll bet that's her now." She swung the door open, revealing a dumbwaiter that held a tray with a large pitcher of lemonade and two glasses.

"You thought some old lady was going to be in *there*?" Rusty asked, aching, alarmed, appalled . . . and absolutely salivating at the mere sight of lemonade.

"Of course. She has arthritis in her knees."

"I know the feeling," he grumbled under his breath, flexing his legs and grimacing.

She took the tray and slammed the door shut with her hip. "How do you think we got you up here? We certainly couldn't have carried you."

"I was in there?" He grew weaker at the thought. "I hate small spaces."

"I know. You didn't like it at all," she stated matter-of-factly. "It was a tight fit too. Come on, and I'll give you some of Miss Lucy's lemonade. You still look a little pale."

"Look, lady," he said, grasping for some semblance of control. "I'm not following you anywhere! I want my shoes, and I want out of here."

"You're in no condition to make demands, Mr. Rivers. You're lucky you aren't in the hospital. Not that I expect any gratitude, mind you."

"*Lady*—" he wailed. "I—I don't know you. I don't know who you are. I don't know where I am. I don't remember getting here, and I sure as hell don't remember getting in that—that contraption. It seems to me that maybe I should have been in a hospital, and you'll be damn lucky if I don't call my lawyer!"

"Mr. Rivers," she said, twirling to face him. "Miss Lucy is thoroughly qualified to handle a case of heat exhaustion, and if I hadn't intervened and rescued you—"

"Abducted, is more like it!"

"—from your own lunacy, you probably *would* be in a hospital at this very minute."

She was so calm. So dad-gummed calm and reasonable and . . . he was so confused. "Look, lady, I don't know who you are or what you're trying to prove. All I know is that I'm getting out of here. Where's the door?"

"Now, let's not be hasty." She raised the tray as if to tempt him. "Try some of this lemonade."

"Lady, I don't—"

"My name is Kevyn."

She smiled, and somehow her smile made her

seem trustworthy. She turned away from him and began gliding down the dim hallway. "Just follow me," she said.

He took a step forward, somehow compelled to follow, intrigued and drawn and . . . "No, dammit—no!"

She stopped short, her slender back a black-clad exclamation point as she pivoted slowly, gracefully, and faced him. *"Mr. Rivers,"* she said, her tone low and cool and aloof, "do not shout at me. Do not curse at me. I am only trying to help you. Is that understood?"

"Not by a long shot. I don't understand a damn thing." His fists clenched at his side. "Who *are* you? And why did you bring me here?" But before she could answer, before he could force her to answer, the room began its slow spin again, his stomach clenched and heaved again, his joints sent screaming protests to his brain again. Only sheer determination kept him from dropping to the floor.

She rested a hand lightly on his arm, and even in the gloom her face seemed to gleam with disturbing intensity. "Why don't we go sit down? You'll feel more comfortable in the parlor, I think." She gave his arm a reassuring pat, then turned and left him to follow. He started to walk, each step a victory over the desire to collapse and rest.

Luckily, she didn't expect him to follow her far. He stepped into the sitting room, bracing his shoulder against the doorjamb. Heavy velvet draperies hung over the windows, shutting out the glare. He had to admit, however grudgingly, that the subdued light was a relief to his burning eyes. He noted her movements as she filled the glasses with lemonade. She handed him one, then sank onto an upholstered chaise lounge that looked like it had survived two world wars—barely.

His legs threatened to give way under him, so he dropped to the camel-backed sofa, exhaling with a weary gasp. He tried to gather his defenses. The room was filled with clutter, which lent it a cozy, though shabby, feeling. Whimsical figurines—unicorns, trolls, and elves—peered at him from shadowy shelves of an old, scarred cherry secretary.

And candles abounded. Dozens of them on every surface: Short ones, tall ones, fat ones, and slender ones. He shivered. The place was a firetrap.

"Why am I here?" he asked in measured tones.

"Partially because I didn't know where else to take you. You weren't wearing any identification. And partially"—she nursed her drink, staring at him intensely—"because I need you."

His fingers tightened on the glass as his pulse stripped gears. He jerked to his feet and edged toward the doorway. "I think I'll go find my shoes now."

"No! Not yet!" She rushed across the room to his side. "Please let me explain. This is very important to me. I have a deadline that—"

"Deadline?" The word hit him like a pail of water. "I should have known!" Slamming his glass down on the table, he turned away from her.

"But I'm willing to pay you," she insisted. "I really need you very badly."

"What is this, some kind of publicity stunt? Sure you need me," he barked out, reality chasing away the eerie fantasy that had gripped him. "You need my name, is more like it."

"Your name? What does your name have to do with it? Not that you don't have a nice name, er, Sergee, but—"

"It's *Sair-gay*. With a hard *g*," Rusty said. "But nobody calls me—"

"All right, Sergei, but I don't need your name, just your body."

"My *what*?" He stared at her, slack-jawed with disbelief. "I'm hallucinating," he muttered. "There's no other explanation for this."

"I'm an artist, Sergei. I want you to model for me. Not nude. I only use professionals for my nudes. And this job doesn't call for a *total* nude, anyway—"

"'Thank God!" he said, remembering the condition he'd awakened in earlier.

"You can't imagine how long I've been looking for my Darius model."

"What kind of scam are you trying to pull?" He backed away from her. "Darius sounds like some kind of Greek or something. I'm no Greek."

"This Darius is an alien."

"Okay, lady. You can play games all you want to, but I don't look Greek *or* alien. If you thought you were going to convince me to do this by batting your baby-blues at me, you can forget it. You want a celebrity? You can go through my agent, just like everybody else. And by the way . . ." He paused. "You can't afford me," he said, emphasizing each word. He eyed possible routes for escape, ready to get out of this place once and for all.

"Agent? You mean, you *are* a model?" She scampered after him as he paced back down the hallway. "That's wonderful! This is so perfect, it's like it was meant to be! I thought you were just another one of those . . . those crazy jocks!"

He froze, the old insult burning through him at lightning speed. "Don't you mean *dumb* jocks?"

"No!" She stood stock-still and stared at him through startled eyes. And then, quietly said, "I would never call anybody that."

"Sure you wouldn't, lady," he muttered.

"It's Kevyn, Kevyn Llewellyn. And I'm sorry. I didn't mean to offend you."

"So you keep telling me, but so far you've done a pretty good job of it. I'm gettin' out of here." He wheeled away from her with as much force as he could muster and strode down the hallway in the direction of the bathroom. "Wait a minute. I don't have to get back in that . . . that *thing*, do I?"

"Why, why—yes," she agreed anxiously.

"You're kidding me."

"The stairs have been boarded up for a long time."

"What?"

"They—they boarded up the inside stairs when they turned the house into a duplex."

"You don't expect me to believe that the only way in and out of this place is—is—there've got to be stairs."

"There are. There were." She stared up at him, and suddenly her face was transformed by a radiant smile. "Termites. Termites ate the stairs last year, and they weren't safe, and after I paid the exterminator, I couldn't afford to have the stairs rebuilt. Which is why this job is so important to me, because once I finish this artwork, I can buy the lumber and pay the carpenters and stop using the dumbwaiter." She stopped smiling and watched him nervously. "You see? That's why I really need your cooperation. I'm running out of time."

"Not running—ran. Out. Gone. And so am I." He retraced his steps to the bathroom. "I'll go through the window."

"There's no ladder!"

"I don't care if I have to tie towels together, lady, I'm getting out of here, and I'm not going in that damned dumbwaiter, and I'm sure as hell not going to wait on the blasted carpenters."

"No!" She flung herself in front of him, blocking the bathroom door. "I can't let you do this. You'll hurt yourself. You need to rest a little longer."

"Lady—"

"Kevyn."

"I'm not at all surprised you have a weird name. You are a weird person. Beautiful, but weird. Too bad. No offense," he added as he peered over her shoulder.

There were only two black velour hand towels hanging beside the sink.

He turned and looked farther down the hallway.

Sheets. Surely she had sheets.

He wheeled away from her and took off down the corridor. The first door was locked. But a beckoning splash of sunlight across the floor at the end of the hall indicated an open door.

Kevyn watched helplessly as her last chance at Darius slipped through her fingers like water through a sieve. Why did he have to be so obstinate? And more to the point, exactly how expensive was he? She needed the money too badly to pay exorbitant modeling fees, but she was too desperate to do much haggling, providing that she could get him to sign the release in the first place.

He halted in midstep and shot a glance toward her. "What's this?" he asked, pointing into the room.

"It used to be a ballroom. Now it's my studio."

Windows and French doors spanned two long walls, allowing the sun's rays to pour in. A stack of canvases leaned against a corner, and several easels held works in progress.

But it was the wall of finished products that seemed to draw him inside. She followed him, hoping that proof of her professionalism, her accomplishments, might soften his attitude toward her project.

He headed straight for the display on the wall: Scenes out of fairy tales—lush forest glades, sparkling waterfalls, earthy grottoes populated with creatures ranging from gargoyles to fairies, all a vivid testimony to the imaginations of the writers whose works she illustrated. But he didn't seem to be admiring *her* work. Instead, he walked straight to the large framed watercolor that was the collection's focal point, the one piece of art that wasn't hers.

A thread of discomfort worked its way through her as he pored over the painting, an ornate work of a young nymph standing in profile amidst a confusion of blossoms, her body draped in gossamer veils, her arms spread out and raised. An exotic butterfly poised for flight, her body was as clearly revealed as if she were nude. Her head was flung back, her hair of ebony and silver-streaked moonlight tumbled down her arched back in a lustrous wave.

"That's you," he stated in a cracked voice, his gaze riveted to the painting.

She shifted her weight uncomfortably. "A friend did it. He was going through an art nouveau period."

"Friend?" He looked at her cautiously, and she suspected that he was trying to determine if her black dress really concealed that body.

"Yes, a friend." She folded her arms across her chest, determined not to show her discomfort. "Simon Killingsworth. Miss Lucy was his grand-mother's second cousin, once removed."

Rusty's face reflected disbelief. "*The* Simon Killingsworth?"

"Yes." She felt a tremor of hope. If he knew of Simon, maybe he'd be impressed enough to give her own project more serious consideration.

"The Simon Killingsworth from London? The one with green hair?"

"Well, he doesn't have green hair anymore, and of course when he painted this he didn't have green hair. And he's not really from London. He's from Bossier City, as a matter of fact."

"I've seen the guy on television. He has a British accent."

"It's an affectation, I'm afraid." She leaned against the wall. "Simon isn't his real name. When we lived together he was Van Kuykendal. Before that, Ralph Beauchamp . . . and so on and so on."

He glared at the painting, and she recognized with a sinking spirit that he wasn't going to be impressed with Simon Killingsworth or probably anything else she had to offer, even money. When he turned and faced her again, she realized she was wrong. Dead wrong. Alarmingly wrong.

His scrutiny robbed her of her breath. His gaze dragged leisurely down her body, pausing at her slender neck, her breasts, her waist, her thighs. Kevyn's poise evaporated. She felt each scandalous inch of the trail his fiery gaze blazed. She was breathless until he finally returned his eyes to hers.

Helplessly aware of how easily he was transposing the imagery of the painting onto her body, and even more helplessly aware of the way her trembling body was reacting to his blatant interest, she felt her pulse skip erratically as the blood tingled through her veins.

She didn't trust her voice to speak. She moved away from the picture that invited comparisons in which she didn't want to participate.

He stepped in front of her and blocked her path. Before she could move around him, he stopped her with a slow grin. "You know, we just might be able to work something out, after all."

"I don't think so." She tried to push past him, but his hand touched her back, his strong fingers applying insistent pressure as his thumbs traced her ribs through the thin black fabric.

"I'm not an unreasonable man," he said in a husky, good ol' Louisiana boy drawl. "You want *my* body . . . and I've decided I want *yours*." Before she could react, he pulled her against him, molding her softness to the hard contours of his bare chest. In his eyes shone an assuredness, a mocking pleasure that staggered her as he continued. "The game looks a little different when we aren't playing by your rules, doesn't it?"

"You've made your point." She placed her hands on his chest to push him away. But his expression changed. His thick lashes lowered, his face drew nearer, and suddenly, quite suddenly, it was no game. He was going to kiss her.

And she had no desire to push him away.

She couldn't breathe, she could only wait, and then . . . then . . . he released her, just when she feared her knees lacked enough strength to hold her upright. It was over, before it had begun.

"Damn." He shook his head in bemusement. "Damn." he repeated.

She tried to convince herself that she would have stopped him from kissing her, if he hadn't stopped first. She tried to convince herself that even now, she wasn't wishing he hadn't stopped. Her hand went nervously to her throat. "You must understand, Mr. Rivers, I don't tolerate this kind of behavior from any of my models. I mean, I can't have you leaving with the wrong impression. I brought you up here for strictly professional reasons." She took a deep breath and pulled herself erect. "You're free to go now, Mr. Rivers. I apologize if my actions have inconvenienced you."

"Mr. Rivers . . ." He studied her face carefully. "You've called me Sergei and Mr. Rivers. You honestly don't know who I am, do you?"

"Sergei Rivers," she responded evenly. "Is that supposed to mean something?"

"Are you telling me that when you picked me up today, you didn't know who I was?"

"Should I?"

He shook his head. "You *don't* know."

Her nerves frazzled to the breaking point, she snapped, "Listen, you may think you're someone special with your 'agent' and your 'high price,' but as far as I can tell, you're just another egotistical jock!"

He recoiled as if she'd slapped him, and then his high cheekbones flushed. "What makes you so sure I'm a jock?"

"Oh, come on," she said. "You were running in a triathlon. And"—she paused significantly, and let her gaze drop down his body—"you certainly didn't develop those pectorals by tap-dancing."

"For your information," he added, "I *am* a dancer."

She raked her gaze over his bare chest, flat abdomen, and firmly muscled thighs. "Uh-huh. And I'm Mamie Eisenhower."

"Lady, I can just about figure what it'd take to convince you, but I'm not in the habit of wearing pink tights and speaking with a lisp."

She stiffened, her chin raising defensively, warily.

A remote smile molded his full, beautifully shaped lips. "You've heard of Alexandra Petrova, I'm sure. Alexandra Petrova *Rivers*?"

"The Russian dancer? Of course, who hasn't?" Kevyn shook her head stubbornly. "No, I don't believe it."

"You don't believe what?"

"I don't know what I don't believe. I just have a feeling that whatever you're going to tell me—I don't believe it."

"She's my mother."

With a sinking feeling, Kevyn stared at his high cheekbones and the foreign appearance that had nagged her all day. No, it wasn't so hard to believe after all. The son of a ballerina of Russian descent . . . Sergei . . . it all added up. Almost.

"Okay. So maybe you're telling the truth." She couldn't keep the grudging tone out of her voice. "Maybe she *is* your mother. But I still say you're no dancer."

"Are you quite sure about that?" His eyes took on the glint of rusty steel, warm in color but cold and threatening in their intensity.

"You don't look like a dancer," she said, but the seeds of doubt were wedged securely in her mind.

He stared at her for a moment that electrified her, that brought the tension between them to a crackling pitch. He squared his shoulders and then turned, pacing deliberately toward the center of the vast hardwood floor.

That walk, she thought disjointedly, watching the sinew and muscles move beneath the surface of his golden-bronze skin, his toes turn out like those of a . . . dancer. "Oh my."

He shook his arms loose, stretching first one leg, then the other. Each movement was fluid yet precise. With a quick snap of his head, he looked at her from over his shoulder and ordered her not to move. She was too spellbound to disobey. He judged the space between them. Then he let his head drop as he inhaled deeply once, twice, and then again, his chest swelling, his hair falling forward over his brow in a thick auburn wave.

With a sudden burst of movement, he performed

a low glide, and with a violent thrust of his powerful legs, he was in the air, soaring with arms outstretched, spinning and landing in front of her. Scant inches of electrically charged air separated them.

"My word," she whispered, awestruck. He reached out and grabbed her hands, jerking them over her head. She felt herself being propelled toward him and tried to protest. But his control seemed born of strength and superb technique, and with a masterful twist of his wrists, he spun her and dropped them both into a dizzying lunge.

Panic-stricken, she was spinning, falling, plunging toward the hardwood floor. Yet the moment of fear was short-lived, as she felt the strength of his arm cradling her back, lowering her swiftly yet safely to his muscled thigh. One hand slid firmly under her waist to keep her from rolling away from him, while the other moved to cup the back of her head as his fingers twined through her hair with a seductive pressure.

He lowered his face until his lips were a mere breath away from hers. When he spoke it was a hoarse whisper, burning with fire.

"Now. Do you believe me?"

Three

Kevyn lay in the arms of her Darius, her breath trapped deep in her throat. Fighting for air, she was unable to tear her gaze away from him. "You . . . you . . ." She shut her eyes in an effort to control her ragged breathing. "You . . . arrogant . . . beast!"

"But do you believe me?" he asked, still holding her in a possessive embrace, sending her blood pressure soaring.

"Yes." She was unable to pull away from him, though whether it was because of his strength or her lack of willpower, she did not know. A soft melting glow dissolved the knot in her stomach. "You shouldn't have done that. Your leg . . ."

"Is killing me," he finished for her. Flinching, he released her, and she slid to the floor. He dropped down beside her, his chest heaving.

"Is there anything I can do to help?" she asked, chagrined for no good reason, since he had done this to himself.

"No." He pulled away. "My trainer will take care of it."

"Trainer?" she said, frowning.

"My—my doctor," he corrected. "It's nothing but a scrape. No muscles or tendons involved." His jaw tense, he reached for his other leg. "At least it wasn't my bum knee. This guy gives me enough hell already."

"Then why in the world were you out there running?"

He shot a glance in her direction and grumbled, "You just don't understand good, healthy competition."

Kevyn leaned forward, a cascade of ebony curls sweeping into her face. "Competition? To prove what?"

He stared at her for a moment, then shrugged it off. "If you don't understand, I can't explain."

"But what you did—it was almost suicidal."

"Let's don't overdo it, okay? It may have been a little foolish, but I'd hardly call it suicidal."

"But you're a dancer. It doesn't fit."

"Don't bet the rent on it, lady." His full lips twisted in a wry grimace. "Dancers compete every day of their lives. Maybe you live in some sort of artistic utopia, but a dance company is a snake pit. Believe me, I know."

"But, Sergei, that's nothing like what you did today."

"Don't—" His head snapped up. "Don't call me that." Then, more calmly, "Not even my mother calls me that."

"What does she call you?"

Two slashes of color stained his high cheekbones, and he concentrated his attention on his thighs. "Just call me . . . Serge."

"I thought you said it had a hard *g*."

"Sergei has a hard *g*. Serge is soft."

"Your mother named you?"

He nodded, kneading his legs like so much tough meat.

"You were named after someone, I'll bet."

"Nobody you've heard of."

"Try me," she prodded.

"Sergei Diaghilev."

"Never heard of him," she admitted.

At first he seemed uninclined to explain, but then he said, almost defensively, "He was the founder of the *Ballets Russes* before World War I."

His voice and tone slipped from Louisiana Southern to exquisite French and back again in the blink of an eye, without his seeming to be aware of it.

"My grandparents danced in his company and got caught in Paris during the Russian Revolution. For obvious reasons, they never went back."

"No wonder you're a dancer." Kevyn felt her cheeks suffuse with heat. "I hope you can forgive me for being so—for doubting your word."

He shifted his weight. "Oh, don't worry about it," he mumbled.

"I understand all about being named after someone. My mother named my oldest brother Heath, after Heathcliff in *Wuthering Heights*, and my other brother Rhett, after—"

"Rhett Butler." He grinned. "Your mother should meet my mother. She's cut from the same cloth."

"She *was*," Kevyn corrected in a low tone of voice. "My parents are dead."

"Oh . . ." He cleared his throat awkwardly. "I'm surprised you weren't named Juliet or Scarlet or something," he finally continued in a teasing voice so different from his earlier tone. "Do you share your mother's taste in books?"

"Oh, no," Kevyn said, startled. "I don't read. I mean . . ." She indicated the wall of artwork. "My interests are much more visual."

"Very."

"My mother wanted to name me Guinevere." Kevyn toyed with the buckle of her sandal. "My father was career Air Force. He wasn't around when either of my brothers were born, so my mother got her way with their names. But I was kind of an afterthought in their lives, after Dad had already retired and Heath was grown and married. Dad put his foot down, said no more of his sons would have sissy names. He insisted that I would be named after a buddy of his who died in Korea. Only I wasn't a son."

"Surprise, surprise."

"But he was too stubborn to back down."

"Kevyn." He tilted his head quizzically. "It's weird, but it fits."

She felt vulnerable, exposed. Her hand went to the neckline of her dress and tangled nervously in the limp red tie.

As if sensing her withdrawal, he changed the subject. "Do your brothers live here in Shreveport?"

"Heath lives in Atlanta. I hardly know him, strange as that may sound." A heavy silence stretched between them, and then, she lowered her eyes. "Rhett died in Cambodia."

"I'm sorry." Rusty reached to brush a strand of hair from her face. But when his fingertips skimmed her temple, he stopped. "Kevyn . . ."

She felt a tremor of awareness that frightened and tantalized her.

"When you kidnapped me—"

"Rescued," she corrected.

"Whatever." He shrugged and continued. "You really must have been desperate to do what you did."

"I was." Dare she hope . . . "I still am."

"What kind of picture did you need?"

"It's for a book cover." She sprang to her feet. "Stay there. I have something I can show you." She crossed to a battered file cabinet and pulled open the top drawer. Luckily Atticus hadn't filed anything for her lately, and the *Darius* information was still up front in its blue color-coded folder. She opened it, stared at the neat stack of pages, and closed it again. She returned to him and presented it. "Everything you need to know is inside."

He opened the folder, his expression bemused. "This is some sort of contract."

"That's my standard model release and contract." *That I hope you'll be signing*, she continued silently. "Keep going. The art description should be there."

He flipped two more pages and then, holding it at arm's length, began reading silently.

"Please," she said. "Read it out loud." At his questioning look, she added, "It helps me visualize."

He squinted slightly. "Sorry, the eyes are going. I usually wear reading glasses. Let's see. . . . Story synopsis?" He glanced at her over the page, and she nodded. " 'Upon the death of his father, Xer— Xer—' "

"Xerxes," Kevyn supplied quickly.

"Xerxes—'See *Xerxes: Defender-King of the Aurelian Galaxy*'?"

"The second book in the Aurelian Dynasty Series. It was nominated for a Nebula last year. I did the cover art on it too."

"Oh." He shrugged and continued, ". . . 'the infant Darius was spirited away to the Gray Planet, where the heavy atmosphere was impenetrable by Gorgolian search-rays and conductive to the development of superior strength and endurance.' " He grinned. "No wonder you need me."

"Go on."

"Sure. 'Endowed with the grace of his mother, the evil Darjeel, and the valor of his father Xerxes, young Darius grew to maturity unaware of his royal heritage or his preordained role in the struggle between Gorgol and the old Aurelian Dynasty, of which he is the sole hope for survival.' " He rubbed the bridge of his nose as he continued to scan the page. "They don't expect much out of him, do they?"

"He dies at the end of the book."

"How do you know?"

"Because it's a multi-book saga, and I'm contracted for three covers—*Xerxes*, *Darius*, and the following book about Darius's daughter, *Aurora: Goddess-Queen of the Aurelian Dynasty.*"

"Well, at least he gets in a little action before he kicks the bucket," he replied with a playful smirk. "But who does him in?"

"Darjeel, of course."

"His own mother?"

"That's the way of things under Gorgol. Of course, only another female has the mental and physical superiority to destroy Darjeel, which brings us full circle, the Aurelian Dynasty restored."

"Your publishers are a sexist lot, aren't they?"

"You have to remember, Xerxes would never have thrown his galaxy into such a mess in the first place, if he hadn't allowed himself to be lured by the Gorgolian siren song. 'Getting a little action,' I believe you called it?"

He let out a disgusted snort and returned his attention to the art facts sheet. Kevyn studied him through half-closed eyelashes. "With the right cover, *Darius* would leap right off the bookshelves and into the buyers' arms."

"You think *I* have that kind of . . . er . . . appeal?"

"To certain members of the buying public, certainly." She refused to give his ego any more to feed on.

"Really?" He seemed too darned pleased with himself.

"As long as they don't know you're a dancer," she retorted. "The image simply wouldn't fit."

"So now we get down to the bottom line." He glowered and shifted his weight to a more comfortable position before raising the page again. " 'Darius: Bearing Aurelian features'—what are Aurelian features?"

"I'll show you in a minute. Go on."

". . . 'with the sturdy musculature of Xerxes, though taller and leaner. He has Darjeel's platinum hair'—" He shot her a confused look.

"Really." Exasperation gave her voice more snap than she'd intended. "Give me a little artistic latitude, okay?"

Frowning, he completed the description that she now knew by heart. ". . . 'hair long and free and unrestrained down his back in primitive Aurelian fashion. Must be unquestionably masculine and powerful, despite hair—remember Laertes fiasco.' " He dropped the sheet to the floor in front of him. "I'm afraid to ask."

"The first book in the series was a disaster. Good book, awful cover. You see, Aurelians never cut their hair. You know, like Samson? Laertes has this long hair, which shouldn't have been a problem, except that he didn't have that—that masculinity, that power that radiated from the canvas. He looked a little dense around the eyes, if you must know the truth."

"I'm very glad to know that I don't look a little stupid around the eyes."

Kevyn laughed in spite of herself. "It was all the artist's fault," she amended quickly. "There was no reason the cover couldn't work, if Fantasy Books hadn't tried to save money and go with a new artist who, luckily for me, hadn't yet developed his talents to be able to do the job." She gave him her most entreating look. "And the first step in doing the job is finding the right model."

"Me." His tone was flat, and not promising.

"Please?" She'd lied, kidnapped, and done everything else in her power. She might as well grovel. She leaped up. "Wait—don't answer yet. I want you to see . . ." She dashed to the other end of the immense room and began flipping through canvases until she found the one she sought. She returned more slowly, for drama's sake, and finally flipped the picture toward him. *"Xerxes."*

She devoured his every expression as he studied the portrait, as his hesitant interest transformed slowly to grudging admiration, and finally to approval. "You do have a way with the male body," he admitted.

"So I've been told." She reached around the front of the canvas to point out *Xerxes*'s hair. "You see, it's thick and shiny, but heavy, and strong enough to make sisal rope out of. Nothing fluffy or feminine about it."

But he wasn't looking at the hair. Instead, he grasped the bottom of the canvas in his hands and adjusted the distance as he examined the emblem in the lower right corner. "What is this?"

Kevyn tugged the canvas free and hurriedly propped it, face away, against the nearest easel. "It's

. . . it's my symbol. A lion rampant, like on the ancient heraldic shields."

"You don't sign your work?"

"That *is* my signature. Llewellyn means descended from lions." She forced nonchalance. "My prints and calendars are quite popular at fan conventions."

"I can see why. They're beautiful." He reached for the folder, and her heart lodged in her throat. "This is a standard contract, you say?"

"Yes. The blanks have to be filled in, of course. And there's your fee to be considered." She spoke cautiously. "I suppose I'd better talk to your agent—that is, if you're interested?"

He seemed a little startled by the question. "Oh, well, I'm sure I could negotiate this without dragging him into it. This isn't exactly his area."

"I suppose not." She finally bit the bullet. "Well, are you going to do it?"

"When's your deadline?"

"Four weeks."

"You really are desperate." A smile, a quite exquisite smile, transformed his features. "I suppose I could help you out."

"You—you will? I mean, you will! Wonderful!" Kevyn lunged for the cabinet and pulled out a 35mm camera before he could change his mind. "Now, if you'd just go stand by the wall and let me get some shots—"

Suddenly, a hard pounding sounded at the front of the house.

Startled, he glanced up at her.

"You don't have to get up," she said quickly. "Just ignore it. It's probably Atticus."

"Who's Atticus?"

"Come on." She tugged at his hand, desperation driving her to frantic measures. "Just let me get a couple of shots—" The pounding continued.

"What's he knocking on?"

"Oh, hell, damn, and double damn!"

He stiffened with suspicion. "Someone's banging on a second-story door that leads nowhere, and Miss

Purity Personified is cursing?" He shifted his weight and began to rise. "Damn," he said with a gasp, "I've tightened up."

"Don't move!" She fled the room, her mind swirling with excuses and fabrications and outright lies—none of which could save her if her "Darius" discovered the excuses, fabrications, and downright lies she'd already used on him. Reaching the door, she jerked it open, ready to hit her nephew with a few well-chosen words. But she found herself face to face with a tall, bearded black man, his fist raised to pound again.

Seeing her, he seemed surprised. "I think I must be at the wrong place."

"Good," she replied, and was about to slam the door, when another voice interrupted her.

"Hey, Kevvie," Atticus said in greeting, and popped out from behind the big man's broad shoulders. "Kevyn, listen to me." He pushed into the room. "One of the athletes disappeared from the race today. A tall, red-haired guy. Somebody at the last aid station said they saw him with a woman who looked like you. I told them that was impossible, but since nobody's been able to find him . . . well, do you have any idea what happened to him?"

The other man stepped forward before she could answer. "You mean, *this* is your aunt? Your old-maid aunt?" As he grinned he pulled a toothpick from his shirt pocket and slipped it into the corner of his mouth. He chewed slowly, his expression amused. "Maybe my man Rusty did drop out of the race, if it had anything to do with this lovely lady."

"Kevyn, this is Skipper Washington. And Skipper, yes, this is my old—my aunt." Atticus flashed a cocky smile at Kevyn.

"I hope you find your friend, but I'm really busy right now. I hate to be rude, but you'll have to excuse me." She glanced nervously over her shoulder, her sins compounding by the minute.

"Kevyn, they clock every entrant as they finish,

and if an athlete drops out, they're supposed to report they're scratching the race."

"They do?" She twisted the tie on her dress until her finger was purple.

"Kevyn, you *do* know something, don't you?"

Damn. If there was anyone in the world who could see right through her, it was Atticus. "He was in trouble, and I heard the first-aid tents were out of ice—"

"Trouble? What kind of trouble?" Skipper demanded. "Where is he?"

It was over. She'd gone through it all, and it was over. Her shoulders slumping with defeat, Kevyn decided that she'd rather face Sergei Rivers's wrath with witnesses. After everything she'd put the poor man through, she wouldn't strike murder totally from his list of options for retaliation. "Serge?" she called sweetly down the hallway. "Someone is here looking for you."

"Serge?" Skipper asked.

"Aren't you looking for Serge Rivers?" she asked, hoping against hope that perhaps two red-haired men had left the race.

"Oh, yeah. Sure. Serge." Skipper nodded, but didn't seem very confident.

At that moment, Sergei Rivers walked into the hall and stopped and stared. "That's a door."

"He *is* in trouble, isn't he?" Skipper asked warily.

Kevyn couldn't do a thing except stand there and wait for Serge to explode.

"I got worried when you didn't finish," Skipper continued, "and this guy, er, Atticus, thought—oh, forget it. I'm just glad to see you're all right."

"Are there stairs outside that door?" Serge asked.

"Well, of course," Atticus responded. "There's no other way up, unless, of course, you count Miss Lucy's dumbwaiter."

At that moment Kevyn could have easily, delightedly killed Atticus. "It's a long story," she singsonged, holding the camera in a choke hold. "And now that you've found him and can take care of him . . ." Her voice dwindled to nothing under

Sergei Rivers's lethal scrutiny. He'd already threatened to call his lawyer, and now she'd lost her Darius as well.

Skipper Washington cocked his head to one side, his eyes twinkling. "Uh, *Serge*?"

Kevyn looked from one man to the other as some silent struggle seemed to transpire between them.

Finally Skipper shrugged his massive shoulders. "You lost the bet." Glancing at Kevyn, he added, "I hope it was worth it, buddy. Besides, our friendly little wager is the least of your problems. It seems the press got word that you were in the triathlon, and Coach and the Colonel found out, and they're pretty burned up about it. They're under the mistaken impression that the team needs you."

"Coach?" Suspicion sizzled through Kevyn. "Team?"

Serge started toward her. "I can explain this."

She pulled away as he approached. "Explain what?"

"You don't know who he is, do you?" Atticus demanded. "I can't believe it! Half the female population of Louisiana would give their eyeteeth to spend the afternoon with this guy, and you don't even know who he is!"

"Since when do you know anything about ballet?" Kevyn asked her nephew.

"*Ballet?*" Atticus and Skipper chorused.

"What's going on here?" Kevyn folded her arms across her waist in a defensive gesture. Serge rubbed the back of his neck and groaned.

"He's a wide receiver for the Louisiana Gents," Atticus explained with exaggerated patience. "You'll have to excuse her, fellas. She doesn't know a football from a golf club."

"She's never heard of the Gents?" Skipper slipped the toothpick from the corner of his mouth. "You've never heard of Rusty Rivers?" Then, in a shocked tone he added, "I'll bet you've never even heard of *me!*"

"Rusty? You mean you even lied to me about your *name*?"

"Well, you lied about the stairs!"

Steaming, Kevyn spun away. "I should have known better!"

"Hey, I had to protect myself." Serge started after her. "I'd been kidnapped by some looney-tunes artist who—"

"*Looney tunes!*"

Atticus motioned to Skipper. "Hey man, she's dangerous when she's upset. We'd better get this guy out of here."

"Kevyn, *please!*" Serge begged.

"Get out of my house this minute! All of you!" Whirling away, she clenched her fists. "A dancer! And I believed him!" A burning ember settled in the pit of her stomach. She felt like such a fool.

Rusty touched her shoulder, but she flinched away.

"I didn't really lie, Kevyn. I *am* a dancer . . . sort of."

"Is that what you call what you do in the end zone?" Skipper asked with a laugh.

"Out!" Kevyn repeated.

"You lied about the stairs!" Rusty yelled. He tried to follow her, but the other men grabbed him by the arms and dragged him through the door.

She stood there trembling for a full minute before she could force any thought into her head to replace the one taunting fact she found most difficult to deal with: He'd made a fool out of her. But another thought was more tormenting, and brought tears of frustration to her eyes. He probably had been laughing at her the whole time.

Strangely enough, the realization that the perfect Darius had slipped through her fingers was the least of her disappointments.

As Skipper hooted with laughter, Rusty hurried down the sturdy wooden staircase last, taking the narrow stairs two at a time and wincing with pain. So he'd lied to her—so what? It was little more than a fib, he told himself as he leaned heavily on the rail at the bottom.

"I'm not leaving without my shoes. She threw them out the damned window." He circled to the back of the house, the others following.

Rusty stared up in impotent rage at the balcony that ran the full circumference of the antebellum home. When she'd tossed his shoes out the bathroom window, she'd obviously known they would land safely on the balcony.

"Hey!" he shouted. "I want my shoes!"

Kevyn's head appeared at the railing. "You want your shoes? Catch!" She hurled them down, and Skipper dodged one while the other bounced off Atticus's shoulder.

Glaring up at her, Rusty shouted, "You know something? You're a nut! A certifiable, card-carrying nut! And I've got news for you—you'd better not use me *or* my body! You do, and I'll sue!"

"Your body?" Skipper demanded. "What were you doing up there?"

"Oh, Lord, is that what all this is about?" Atticus moaned. "Darius. I should have guessed. Well, I don't know about you-all, but I'm not waiting around to see what she throws next." He took off for the parked cars, the others following close on his heels.

Rusty sank back into the passenger's seat of Skipper's car and groaned. He buried his face in his hands. "I think I'm gonna be sick."

Skipper shot him a worried look. "What happened back there?" he asked.

"What happened? What do you mean, what happened? *Nothing* happened."

Skipper's laughter was devilish. "Something happened, all right. I've never seen you so shook up."

"Of course I'm shaken up. That crazy dame made me lose our bet, which I have no intention of paying, dammit! I would've finished if she hadn't kidnapped me—"

"You'll pay, buddy, one way or another. But right now, you've brought up an interesting point. Since when could a sweet little thing like that manhandle you?"

"I was in no condition to argue. I was delirious with exhaustion."

"You looked okay when I got there. In fact, you looked mighty cozy. Didn't seem to be making any moves to leave that I could tell."

"The sun got to me, that's all," Rusty said several minutes later.

"Uh-huh."

Rusty's head snapped up. "Well, you don't think it had anything to do with that—that—"

"She sure has pretty eyes, doesn't she? I've never seen eyes that color," Skipper remarked.

"I didn't notice."

"Of course, she was probably wearing contact lenses."

"She wasn't wearing contacts." Rusty scowled at the sparkle in his friend's eyes. He jerked his head around to stare out the window again. "I noticed, okay? How could you not notice a woman who looks like that? But that silver stuff on her hair—those streaks? They must be artificial. I tell you, the lady is weird."

Rusty prodded his knee, hoping he hadn't done any irrevocable damage executing that damned *tour jeté*. Noticing the corner of a scarf peeking out from under the seat, he pulled it free and held it in his hands, allowing the sheer silk to caress his roughened palms. Soft muted intensities of aquamarine and silver bled together with alabaster white, reminding him of gossamer veils and willowy bodies. . . . As the feather-light scarf slid over his fingers he felt the blood surge through him, and his mind was incapable of erasing the enticing vision. Stifling a curse, he crumpled the fabric into a ball and flung it to the floor.

"Hey, man! Careful with that scarf. My girlfriend paid a hundred bucks for it if she paid a dime!" Skipper shook his head sadly. "That woman sure can spend money!"

But Rusty wasn't listening. "It must have been the sun." He groaned softly.

Four

Rusty yawned, sipped his coffee, then positioned the mug between his legs and started his car. He dreaded sitting through this early team meeting before morning practice. His muscles burned; his knees throbbed. But if he betrayed his aches and pains by even a wince, Coach Bigelow's wrath and fury would crash down upon his aching shoulders. He clenched the gearshift.

Then there was the strange woman who was the source of his sleepless night . . . and if he didn't get her out of his head, she might shatter his ability to concentrate completely. She had seemed so driven, so desperate, and so damned relieved and grateful when he'd almost succumbed to her nonsense.

Hoping to blow some of the cobwebs out of his head, he flipped on the radio as he pulled out onto Lakeshore Drive.

"—mornin', early birds, this is KPOP Shreveport-Bossier City, on a bright and beautiful August morning. Locals have been following the on-field heroics and off-field antics of former Byrd High School standout Rusty Rivers for years. This weekend the talented twenty-nine-year-old wide receiver further demonstrated the kind of professional disregard that has gotten him cut or traded from the Washington Redskins, the Buffalo Bills, and the Phoenix Cardinals."

Rusty's knuckles whitened on the steering wheel.

"Not only did he compete in the grueling Annual

Cross Lake Triathlon on Saturday—a possible breach of contract involving his 'unnecessary risks' clause—but he also disappeared for several hours, causing officials and friends much concern. He was located later at an undisclosed location."

Rusty hurled a particularly pungent barnyard epithet. Another voice came over the air.

"Goodmorning-goodmorning-goodmorning-goodmorning!" the gratingly familiar voice chimed. *"This is Atticus 'Atta-boy' Llewellyn, your number one deejay on your number one station, KPOP, here to get the good times a'rollin' on both sides of the Red River. This morning we'll be hearing from Madonna, Whitney Houston, and Billy Joel. . . . But, first, I've got a football scoop of my own. It's not often that the 'golden throat' gets the jump on the boys in the newsroom, but today I've got an exclusive. More about it after this word from Bonaparte's Cajun Fried Catfish."*

"So help me . . ." Rusty snarled as the theme song for Gents owner Colonel Bonaparte's nationwide catfish franchises filled the car, "if you so much as open your mouth about last Saturday, I'll 'Atta-boy' your teeth right down your throat."

"So, you're wondering about Rusty Rivers's sudden vanishing act only one week before the Gents' first preseason game? You will be relieved to know, it wasn't a sudden case of cold feet—he was kidnapped! Yes, you heard me right—abducted—by none other than my old maid aunt!" His laughter sounded downright maniacal to Rusty's burning ears. *"I know what you're thinking,"* the deejay continued. *"The old lady ought to be locked up, and I suppose you're right . . . but, we have to catch her first!"*

The opening bars of "Little Ol' Lady From Pasadena" jarred through the speakers.

Rusty slammed on his brakes. Hot coffee sloshed onto his chino slacks, stinging his thighs. "I ought to sue that son of a—" he started, but a pickup truck behind him honked, halting his wishful thinking. He accelerated with more weight on the pedal than necessary, rolled down his window, and slung the remaining coffee out.

He was wide awake now.

Kevyn studied her sketches through weary eyes.

She still didn't have a model, and even if Serge—Rusty—hadn't refused to sign a model's release, she finally admitted that perhaps he was wrong for Darius after all. But if so, what was she going to do? And what had muddled her judgment? How could she have been so wrong?

The man's memory haunted her. It didn't make sense. His features should have lent themselves easily to platinum tresses. But the preliminary sketch she had done was lifeless on the page until she stroked the edge of a burnt-sienna artist's crayon across his hair. That change alone had given him a vibrant new dimension.

A familiar rhythm of banging at the door interrupted her thoughts. She sank onto a wicker chair, anger flaring through her as Atticus swung into the room.

"Kevvie, I've been knocking and knocking, and you don't answer."

"I don't suppose it would ever occur to you that I didn't want to see you."

"Not want to see me?" He seemed genuinely intrigued by the idea, then shook his head. "Nah, impossible. Did you hear my show this morning?"

She closed the sketch pad and slid it under her chair, then poured some tea into his cup and handed it to him. "I never listen to you. You know that."

Atticus breathed an audible sigh of what seemed suspiciously like relief. Resting his head against the wall, he asked, "How did Rusty Rivers end up here the other day?"

"I don't want to talk about it." Her sharp tone of voice was enough to stall even the most intrepid nephew. "And Atticus, you'd better not say a word about that visit on the radio. Not one word, do you understand?"

The corner of his mouth twitched. He was up to something, and Kevyn had no time or patience for any of his somethings this day.

"You know, this is a ratings week." Atticus blithely stirred honey into his tea. "I'm doing my best to keep up listener interest. If we pick up another two points, my job'll be secure for a long time, not to mention the big raise I've been promised."

"Not one word," she repeated. *"Do you understand?"*

"Yes," he finally said. "I understand. Anyway, I'm here on business."

"You're not modeling for Darius, and that's final."

"That can wait. *My* business first. I need you to do me a favor. A really big favor." His expression was beseeching, altogether too calculated a look to affect her after all these years.

"This doesn't sound promising." Kevyn crossed her legs and sipped her lukewarm tea, preparing herself for one of Atticus's ridiculous requests.

"Oh, it isn't that bad. I have a public appearance in a few weeks, and I need a date."

"That shouldn't be a problem."

"I need *you*."

Kevyn sliced a warning glance toward him. "Now, *that's* a problem. Forget it. You know I don't like crowds and public places."

"You were in one on Saturday."

"That was important."

"So's this."

"Atticus, please don't push me." She glared at her nephew, blaming him silently for more problems than he knew existed.

"It's for charity, Kevyn. Just think of all the starving children in India. Or was it Nepal?" His brow furrowed in confusion.

Kevyn shot him a withering look. "If they took all the money they're going to spend on liquor, entertainment, and clothes, and donated *that* to charity, they could feed all the starving children in India *and* Nepal."

"You just don't understand."

"That's right. I don't understand."

Atticus idly picked a speck of lint from his trousers. "Don't let the fact that I've never let *you* down influence you."

Kevyn fought the urge to throttle him. "Believe me, I won't."

"Or of course, that without my help you'd never understand the first word of those contracts you have a habit of signing."

"Don't push your luck," she snapped back. "It's one of 'those contracts' that has me in a dither right this very moment."

"Kevyn, that's not the real reason, and you know it." He rose to his feet. "So, where's the mail?"

"I forgot to get it. It's still on top of the filing cabinet." She trailed behind him as he made his way to the studio. "Most of it's junk, I know. I haven't had a chance to sort through it."

"Thank goodness. Last time you sorted your own mail you threw away your credit card because you thought it was junk."

"Some loss. I never use it. I wouldn't have the thing if you hadn't insisted."

"Someday you may find yourself in so desperate a situation that you'll be grateful for that wretched little piece of plastic—even if you do have to sign your name with people watching."

Kevyn stiffened, but Atticus seemed not to notice. He flipped through a week's worth of mail, tossing most of it. Finally he held only three envelopes. "Your gas bill, a newsletter, and . . ." He flourished the last envelope. "More information from Kurzweil."

"Oh, Atticus!" she said excitedly. She leaped forward and tore it from his hand. She opened the envelope with trembling fingers. Several fliers fell out, along with a cover letter. "Here." She thrust the letter at him and then began examining the photo illustrations on the first flier.

"Hey, Kevvie, you're in luck." His hand on her shoulder drew her attention away from the coveted electronic equipment she was drooling over. "Kurzweil is having a demonstration of their Personal Reader in Baton Rouge in two weeks. Why don't you let me take you?"

"Oh, I don't think so, Atticus." She rolled her shoulders edgily. "I don't really need to see a demonstration of the machine. It was *made* for people like me. Besides, I have to do the Darius painting and . . . and . . ." Suddenly the reality of her situation took glorious root in her heart, and she felt the beginnings of exhilaration bubbling in her veins. "Do you realize what this means? With the money from Darius, I'll have enough to buy my own Personal Reader. Why do I need a demonstration? I'll have my own."

"You already have the best personal reader available. Me. So why don't you just give *me* that ten thousand dollars, and . . ." He broke off and gave her shoulders a squeeze. "I'm thrilled for you, Kev. You've worked hard and waited a long time for this."

"A long time," she agreed.

"Kevyn," he said softly. "About those starving children . . ."

"I've already given you my answer." But he had her, and they both knew it. Lord knew, he had never hesitated to help her, regardless of how inconvenient it may have been.

Grasping at straws, she offered unconvincingly, "I don't have anything to wear."

"What about that satin thing? You know, the one you wore in London at the World Fantasy Convention."

"This affair is that dressy?"

"I'm wearing black tails. We'll look fabulous. Stunning. Dramatic." He cocked his head. "Won't we?"

Kevyn struggled but couldn't help responding to his bulldozer ebullience. "We'll be positively smashing, and you'd better appreciate this, because I'm going to hate every minute of it."

Three weeks later on Saturday night Atticus arrived, resplendent in a classic black tuxedo, complete with tails and cape. He took her hand and twirled her, inspecting the effect of her ebony satin dress with its widely ruffled neckline, scooping low yet remaining firmly within the bounds of propriety. It was a dress that caressed not clung, that revealed much yet concealed more. With obvious approval, he moved her to face the mirror. "You look dynamite. *We* look dynamite. It's a shame I've told everyone I'm bringing my aunt. We could pass for twins."

"Everyone?" She felt a tremor of unease as she swept her free-flowing mane of hair over her shoulders. "Something's going on here . . ." She turned to face him, but his countenance was suddenly as innocent and boyish as ever, his head cocked in question.

"Why, Auntie dear, whatever do you mean?"

"Why do I let you talk me into these things?" she asked edgily.

With a flamboyant flourish, he offered his arm. "Shall we go?"

A few people were milling around in the hallway outside the Crystal Ballroom of the Sheraton Pierremont, wearing three-piece suits and dinner dresses.

"Atticus," she murmured nervously, "I thought you said this was a formal affair."

"I said I wanted to make a dramatic impression. And we do, don't you think?"

After checking his cloak, Atticus swept Kevyn into the ballroom. If the expressions on the other guests' faces were any indication, Atticus's arrival had achieved exactly the effect he desired; exactly the effect Kevyn dreaded. They were the focused attention of every person in the room. Kevyn heard the whispered comments pass through the crowd.

But Atticus was clearly in his element as he chatted through the introductions, making enough small talk for both of them. Ever the considerate nephew, he placed a glass of champagne, which Kevyn had no intention of drinking, in her hand.

A short, burly man appeared at Atticus's elbow. His back was ramrod stiff, his iron-gray flattop a dead giveaway of military background. "You're late. But I can certainly understand why." He took Kevyn's hand in his. "And of course, Atticus, my boy, you have the most beautiful woman in the room on your arm."

Overdressed and looking like a complete fool was more like it, Kevyn thought despairingly, terrified that the man could feel her hand trembling in his.

"Colonel Bonaparte, how are you?" Atticus said. The colonel released Kevyn's hand to shake Atticus's. "Kevyn, Colonel Bonaparte is one of my show's primary sponsors. And of course, Kevyn is the aunt you've heard me speak of so often."

The Colonel fixed his no-nonsense gaze square upon Kevyn, and she suddenly felt like a moth pinned on velvet for display. "But you are the aunt who kidnapped Rusty Rivers?"

Kevyn's crystal facade cracked. Her fingers tightened on the stem of the glass.

The Colonel laughed heartily. "That bit was terrific publicity. I've had any number of people ask me about it, which is a hell of a lot better than being asked about our preseason losses."

"I'm glad you appreciated it, sir." For once, Atticus seemed unsure of himself, as Kevyn stared at him in confusion and dismay. "Now, Kevyn, don't look at me like that. It was a joke, that's all. Ratings week, remember?"

She swallowed hard, raising her chin a notch, "I'm sure it was very clever." Before anyone could fill her in with the gory details, Kevyn added, "I'm sorry. If you'll excuse me, I'm . . . I'm afraid I'm not feeling well." She wasn't. Lord knew she wasn't. She slipped away from them, straight into the crush of people.

She was unaware that Atticus had followed her until he grabbed her elbow and tried to halt her.

"Atticus." Her voice was trembling despite her best efforts to control it. "I—I'm ready to leave. *Now*."

"All right. There's no need to get upset." He pried her fingers from the champagne glass in her hand and gulped the now-flat wine down.

"You were talking about me and—and Rusty Rivers—on the radio? Exactly what did you say?"

"Nothing much. Nothing to worry your pretty little head over."

"Don't patronize me." She tried to brush past him.

"Kev, first let me explain. It's not anything like the way it sounds. The 'old-maid aunt' bit is a running gag that doesn't have anything to do with you." Atticus grabbed her elbow. "I'm sorry, Kev. I had no idea it would upset you so much. Just wait here while I get my cloak, and I'll take you home."

"Don't bother. I can take a cab." She squeezed her eyes closed for a brief moment, then opened them again. All she wanted was to get out of there. Staring . . . everyone was staring at her.

Waiting for Skipper to make his own exit from the ballroom, Rusty bent over his drink at the bar in Jacque's, the Sheraton's lounge.

He toyed guiltily with the ice in his highball. He had stuck out the fund-raiser, signing autographs and listening to old high school football stories as long as he possibly could. But he didn't feel like socializing. He felt downright surly, if the truth were known.

Rusty's muscles were knotted with tension beneath his tweed sports coat, a tension he carried around like an extra set of shoulder pads. Coach Bigelow had been riding him at practice, his knee was acting up, they'd lost all their preseason games, and Sunday's season opener—Lord, the season opener. Talk about humiliation.

He cupped one hand over his forehead, shutting out the crowd, the distractions, but he couldn't shut out the flashing images. And damn it all, the recurring image was *that woman.*

Damn. He gulped his drink down. Maybe he needed to see her for real. That day had been so weird, he'd probably overreacted, imagined her effect on him to be stronger than it actually was. He dragged his fingers through his hair, ruffling its unruly waves, trying to stifle his frustration. He considered ordering another drink, but didn't. Enough was enough.

He shoved his empty glass away and swiveled on the stool. Propping his elbows on the counter behind him, he stared sullenly at the lobby, at the people passing by. Where was Skipper?

And to his amazement, *she* was there . . . raven haired, sleek bodied, gorgeous. He could see her, smell her, almost taste her. Damn! How strong had that drink been? He took a deep breath to clear his head.

She was still there.

Her nose was slightly tilted upward, as regal as a duchess's. Even from a distance he was struck by the appearance of porcelain skin against black satin, of her cloud of glossy black, silver-streaked hair.

Rusty slid off the stool in a fluid movement and worked his way through the crowded bar. He stepped into the lobby. "Look at me, dammit," he muttered under his breath.

She had to feel it—that intense sensation pulling him nearer. Of course she felt it. It shimmered in the air between them. She came closer, gliding toward him with the innate grace he remembered so well. But still she didn't see him.

She was walking past him, across the lobby. The clean click of her heels against the tile sounded louder to him than any other noise in the hotel.

With a few loping strides, he crossed the space between them and touched her arm. She whirled toward him, her eyes opening in a burst of cloudy teal blue that took his breath away.

"Fancy meeting you here," he drawled, his lips slipping into a too-easy, too-practiced good ol' boy grin to hide the confusion churning inside of him.

"I . . . I beg your pardon?" She darted a distressed glance around them, then back at him, and for a moment, for one unbelievable moment, he could have sworn she didn't recognize him.

"I'm the perfect body, remember?"

"M—Mr. Rivers," she stammered, and he felt the world jog back into its normal orbit. "I'm sorry. I—I was just leaving." She moved away from him with a rustle of black satin.

"Aw, come on." Rusty stepped quickly in front of her, blocking her path. "I just want to talk to you a moment."

But she shrank from him, causing him to stop short, to follow her distracted gaze over his own shoulder.

And then, before he could make sense of her reaction, she turned to her escort. "Atticus, please . . . I told you to stay and finish your business."

Atticus. Rusty heard a replay of that golden-throated voice chortling words such as "kidnapped" and "abducted." "You . . ." Rusty felt every whiskey-languid muscle in his body slowly tense and his hands curl into balls. A week's frustration seemed to crystallize before him in the human form of Atticus Llewellyn. "Just the guy I've been wanting to see."

The deejay curled his arm protectively around Kevyn's shoulders. "Not tonight, man."

Almost before Rusty could react they were walking away from him, plowing straight into a crowd of people, Atticus grinning and waving to a photographer as a strobe flashed. Without thinking, Rusty sprang forward. "I don't think you understand," he said, his voice crackling with strain, with frustration. The deejay glanced back at him, seemingly surprised that Rusty was still there. "If you and your radio station don't lay off of me . . ." Rusty began, groping for a threat that didn't sound ludicrous, or worse, criminally threatening. He raised his hand to make a point. What point? He wasn't sure. The expression on Atticus Llewellyn's face transformed from mildly annoyed to shocked, and Rusty realized—too late—that it was a fist he'd raised, a trembling fist. What was wrong with him? How much had he had to drink? The deejay shoved Kevyn aside, drew his fist back and—

This is crazy, Rusty wanted to protest, but fist met chin. Rusty was aware of two things: excruciating pain as four knuckles rammed into his tender under-jaw, and an expression of pure horror on Kevyn's beautiful, stunningly beautiful, gloriously beautiful face. For hours he would believe that he had actually seen stars.

Five

"No!" Kevyn cried.

A strobe flashed, exploding like fireworks as Rusty teetered before crashing to the floor. Kevyn shrank back as they were suddenly surrounded by gawking people. The man with the cameras slung around his neck angled this way and that for a better shot.

Atticus flexed his mangled fist, then bent over the football player on the floor. He gaped at Kevyn and demanded in awe, "Did I do that?" And then, before Kevyn could answer, he swung toward the camera, shrugged, and raised his hands in mock-innocence. "Hey, you saw it. Self-defense, right?"

She couldn't breathe, couldn't move. Even the sounds around her seemed muffled by her confusion. Rusty was sprawled at her feet. She had to do something. She had to help him. If only they would all leave her alone—leave him alone.

Then Skipper Washington lunged through the crowd, a full head taller than most of them.

"Hey man, this . . . this isn't what it looks like," Atticus insisted. "He came after me."

Skipper looked down at Rusty. Then he grabbed Rusty by the collar of his jacket and dragged his prone body across the floor toward the front door.

Kevyn backed away from the crowd, her damp palms flattened against the heavy satin skirt to still their trembling. Her earlier anger at Atticus over his publicity-seeking schemes was mild compared to the terror she felt now. Pushing through the crowd while Atticus defended himself and, yes, showed off for the press, she hurried away.

Distress quaked through her body. When a uniformed doorman flung open the heavy glass doors, she darted through them.

Spying the line of limousines awaiting their owners' return, she walked calmly to the first in line. The startled chauffeur stared, his mouth gaping, as the doorman opened the door and Kevyn lunged inside, pressing desperately into the far corner of the plush backseat. She watched the retreating figure of the uniformed doorman through the window. The photographer pushed through the hotel doors, casting predatory looks up and down the walkway.

"Please," she whispered. "Please get me out of here! I'll pay you . . ."

"I guess I've got a couple of hours." He started the limo and pulled away from the curb. "Just tell me where you live, ma'am." He shook his head in bemusement, smiling sympathetically at her in the rearview mirror. "Never let it be said that I refused to help a lady. My mamma would tan my hide!"

"Thank you," Kevyn murmured, blinking back tears. "Thank you, so much . . ."

Rusty stretched, then winced at the pain in his jaw. His eyes blurred shut with sandy residue from sleep, he ran his knuckles over the bruised area and groaned. In addition to the heavy morning stubble, he felt a tender swelling. Who'd have thought a guy like that . . . that *deejay* could carry such a wallop?

The telephone jangled on the nightstand. He rolled over and groped for it. "Yeah," he croaked into the receiver. But the voice at the other end brought him to full attention. He straightened, running his fingers through his hair. "Oh, yeah. Hi, Mom."

"*Mon chou,* what is this I am reading?"

"I can't see through the phone, Mom," he grumbled. "You tell me and we'll both know."

"You are hurt, *chéri*?" Her voice lilted through the receiver.

"No, Mom. I'm fine. Why shouldn't I be?" He rubbed his jaw. She must have radar . . . "Wait a minute, what *are* you reading?"

"*Le journal*—the newspaper—you have seen it, have you not?"

"No." A cold fist of alarm squeezed his gut at the urgency in her voice. "Mom, what is it? Have I been cut from the team? Damn!" He slammed his fist against the headboard. "They can't do that, not right before we play the Saints!"

"Oh, Rusty, you must get your mind out of the football field. It is so hot, and I have a class to teach in a few moments." She sighed. "Perhaps you should read the newspaper yourself, then call me. Or perhaps you can come visit? I *must* hear of this divine creature. *Au revoir.*"

Rusty lay there for a moment, listening to the dial tone humming in his ear, trying to make sense out of her bizarre conversation.

"Wait a minute." He sat straight up. "What divine creature?"

Suddenly, he was throwing the receiver down with one hand, grabbing a pair of running shorts with the other, jerking them over his thighs and hips, and stumbling toward the front of the house. When he swung the front door open, he winced blearily at the glare. He seized the newspaper from the front step and stepped back inside.

The rubber band snapped as he ripped the paper open and saw the photo on the front page. Stunned, he slid down the door until he was sitting on the floor. "Oh, *merde* . . ."

Kevyn slung her brush into the can of turpentine, splashing its mud-colored contents onto the drop cloth on the floor. Nothing held her attention. The Darius project had jinxed her from the start.

Footsteps on the stairway startled her out of her

solitude. The jaunty clattering was easily recognizable. Before the French doors swung open, she was positioned to face her nemesis.

"Atticus Llewellyn, don't you set foot in this house or I'll—"

"Have you seen the morning paper?" he demanded, setting both feet inside the house, one after the other. "It's fantastic! Front-page coverage. Better than I ever dreamed!" He handed her the newspaper. "Listen to the caption—'Confederacy Falls Again!' Beautiful!"

Kevyn snatched the paper away from him and studied the appalling photograph: Rusty Rivers lay sprawled on the floor; Atticus hovered over him; Kevyn stood between them, her confused expression revealing none of the horror that had raced through her at that moment—and at this one.

"And there's more on page 12B." Atticus began rustling through the pages in his hands. "Listen, I'll read it to you."

"No!" She crushed the paper against her body. "I don't want to hear it!"

He raised his startled gaze to hers. "Don't you think you're overreacting to this? They spelled your name right and everything."

Her voice deadly calm, Kevyn clutched the crumpled pages. "I suppose I'll have to take your word for that, won't I?"

He raised a placating hand. "Kevyn, if you'd just let me read it to you—it's really funny."

"Don't you understand?" Her eyes filled with tears. "It doesn't *feel* funny to me."

"Oh, jeez. Kev, I—I'm sorry. It's not nearly as bad as you're thinking."

She turned her back to him, her body trembling. "Atticus, *please*. I can't talk about it. Just leave me alone."

"Okay, okay. I'll come back later when you've calmed down."

She didn't move until she heard the door quietly close behind him. Then she rushed to the kitchen and grabbed the telephone. She could hardly dial the number. As she waited through the rings, she forced herself to look at the newspaper again; letters swam across the page in a jumble, like gears sprung from a disastrously broken clock. An old, familiar frustration closed over her heart as she crushed the paper into her fists.

Miss Lucy answered.

"It's me, Kevyn. Do you have this morning's paper? Would you—would you read me what it says about—about Atticus and me?" She gulped a deep breath. "And Rusty Rivers?" she added with a belated whisper.

Miss Lucy went to find the paper and Kevyn pressed her cheek against the cool refrigerator to calm herself. Demon, her cat, squinted down at her from on top of the refrigerator, then stepped gingerly onto his favorite perch—her shoulders. She gave an exasperated sigh at his intrusion, then grudgingly reached up to scratch the top of his head.

And somehow, with his purr in one ear and Miss Lucy's gentle reading voice in the other, she managed to convince herself that those other voices, those hurtful, laughing voices didn't matter.

The footsteps on the stairway an hour later elicited a groan from her lips. This tread had grown familiar too. Heavy, steady—Bobby Ray, her model for Darius.

"Hey," he said when she opened the door. "I just thought I'd drop by and see how the picture's comin'." Muscles rippling in his arm, he jerked a soggy sweatband from his shaggy blond hair.

She stepped aside to give him a clear view of the canvas.

"Wow." He stood stock-still in the doorway, his face a study first of surprise, then undisguised pride. "Wow!"

"It's almost finished."

"Wow . . ."

Kevyn's face relaxed into a smile. "I suppose I can take that as a compliment."

"That's not my hair, though."

"This isn't a picture of you, it's a picture of a character in a book. And in the book the character has long hair. It's part of his culture—never to cut his hair, for fear of losing his manhood."

"You know," he said, concentrating on his own likeness. "You made my right pec bigger than my left."

"You're the only one who'll notice. Besides," she cocked her head. "No body is perfectly symmetrical. Your right pectoral muscle *is* bigger than your left."

"You've gotta be kidding! Where's a mirror?"

"Oh, good grief, Bobby Ray. Don't be silly." But seeing his concerned expression, she relented. "Oh, all right. Use the big mirror in the bathroom, if you don't believe me. And while you're at it, wash your face with cool water. You look like you're on the brink of heatstroke—"

She broke off, caught off guard by the sudden image of another heat-stricken warrior–god.

The sound of footsteps, the third set that day, caused her to stop. Not a clattering like Atticus's, or a heavy tread like Bobby Ray's, but footsteps with a slightly uneven rhythm and cadence all their own.

A firm knock snapped her out of her momentary stall. She moved forward and swung the door open.

His auburn hair slightly ruffled, his muscles not bulging like Bobby Ray's but so very much *there*, Rusty stared down at her.

"What do you want?" she demanded, more sharply than intended.

"A little courtesy for starters."

"I gave at the office." She started to push the door shut.

He reached out and caught it, gently but firmly pushing it back open. Producing a neatly folded newspaper from under his arm, he stepped in. "I need to talk to you."

She raised her chin, feeling the blood drain from her face. "I know about the paper, and I don't want to discuss it. I appreciate your concern, but I'm really very busy—"

"Kevyn . . ." Bobby Ray appeared at her shoulder, his furry chest bare, rubbing his damp hair with a black towel. "Oh, sorry. I didn't mean to interrupt."

"You didn't." Kevyn and Rusty spoke simultaneously.

"Aren't you Rusty Rivers?" Bobby Ray asked genially. "Hey, man—you are! I can't believe it! Me, meetin' Rusty Rivers." He extended his right hand, and Rusty hesitated for a split second before taking it.

"I see this isn't a convenient time," Rusty remarked. "And since you already knew about the paper, I won't stay."

"Well, isn't that a coincidence?" Bobby Ray asked. "I was just thinking of runnin' along myself. Do you think you could give me a lift? I'm a big fan of yours. Have been since you played for the Redskins."

"Sorry. I'm not going in that direction."

"You don't know which direction—"

"I'm not going that way."

"Oh." The blond shrugged. "Well, that's all right. How's that knee of yours? Still acting up?"

"Listen," Kevyn inserted firmly. "You two can visit all day, for all I care. But I've got a deadline. So, if you'll excuse me, I'm going back to work."

"Oh, don't worry about me," Bobby Ray insisted. "I really was gonna leave, anyway." He grabbed his T-shirt and started for the door. "It was great meeting you, Rusty. And Kevyn, I'll check the picture out again, maybe in a couple of days?"

Kevyn could only manage a nod in reply. She arched a glance at Rusty, but he made no move to follow. Avoiding his gaze, she left the room. To her distress, Rusty followed her.

She turned to find him leaning against the door-jamb. "I'm sorry if I ran him off."

"Bobby Ray is my model," she explained stiffly.

He jerked his thumb toward the canvas in the studio. "That's not the way I pictured it."

Me either, as you should well know, she wanted to say.

"And you called me a dumb jock?"

"I *never* called you that," she corrected him emphatically. "And Bobby Ray is not dumb. He's very successful, if you ask me."

"At what?" Skepticism tinged Rusty's voice.

"He has developed his main asset—his body, of course—into a very satisfying career. He's a body trainer at Atticus's health club." She couldn't refrain from adding wickedly, "He's done wonders for Atticus's upper body strength, wouldn't you say?" She could tell her barb had hit home by the color in Rusty's cheeks—that lovely ruddiness that seemed to betray his best efforts at containing his emotions.

"I didn't realize you appreciated brute strength and physical prowess," he finally remarked pointedly.

"I appreciate people who make the best of the hand that's dealt them." And then, belatedly, she added, "Forgive me. I haven't asked you why you're here."

"After last night, I felt like I owed you some kind of an apology." He hooked his thumbs into his back pockets. "I really wasn't going after that guy—after Atticus. Things kind of went crazy, and the next thing I knew, I was in the backseat of Skipper's car. I feel kind of mixed-up, to tell you the truth. I just wanted to talk to you. I don't understand what happened."

"It wasn't your fault." She averted her gaze. "I—I wasn't feeling well. I just couldn't talk to you."

"You didn't look sick. You looked . . ." He seemed to grope for a word, and then said, almost surprised at the thought, "You looked afraid." He stepped closer to her. "You feel it, too, don't you? You're afraid of what's happening between us."

"I don't know what you're talking about." She took a step back to counter his move. "I . . ." Suddenly, she found herself speaking the truth instead of excuses. "I don't like crowds. I had to get out of there. That was all that I could think of—getting out of there." She forced a dry swallow.

"I don't understand it," he said slowly, "but I believe it. You were really panicked, weren't you?"

"Yes. I was." She couldn't bring herself to meet his gaze.

He wouldn't allow her to avoid it.

His knuckle brushed her chin, then raised it, until she found herself unable to look anywhere but into his woodsy-green eyes. "But now, there aren't any crowds around, Kevyn Llewellyn." He touched the corner of her eye. "You can't tell me you don't feel something happening between us now, can you?" He seemed just as fascinated, just as entranced, just as breathless as she when he dragged a fingertip down her cheek, stroked her neck. "Are you going to tell me you don't feel it?"

She couldn't tell him that, damn him. She couldn't form words at all. She could only respond to the tingles his merest touch sparked.

"I rest my case."

"What do you want from me?" she asked hoarsely.

"All the way over here, I asked myself that very question. And now, I know the answer. I want to start over. I want to pretend we don't have a whole truckload of personality clashes behind us and start over. I want someone to introduce us, and say something like 'Kevyn Llewellyn, this is Rusty Rivers, faster than a speeding bullet, able to leap tall safeties with a single bound.' "

"What's a safety?" she asked, relieved at any opportunity to redirect the thread of his conversation, and intrigued despite her firmest resolutions not to be.

"A kind of football player. Someone whose sole purpose in life is to bust up my plays and"—he glanced down—"my knees."

"Sounds like a nice guy."

"Then I'd want them to say," he went on, " 'Rusty, this is Kevyn Llewellyn, painter of whimsy, spinner of dreams, with eyes that . . ." His voice drifted off, and he closed the distance between them. "The most beautiful eyes I've ever seen in my life . . ."

Dangerous. A prickling sensation danced across her skin as his voice stroked over her.

"Then I imagine this someone who was introducing us would say, 'I realize that you two have absolutely nothing in common. But who the hell cares? Why don't you get to know each other? Who knows? You might even *like* each other' . . ."

Very dangerous. She couldn't think or even breathe under his close scrutiny.

"Well, what do you think?"

"Think about what?" she choked out.

"Do I get to stay?"

How had he gotten so close? Straining for a natural tone, she brushed her hair back and faced him. "I'm not sure."

"It'll give us a chance to get to know each other. You can ask me anything you like. Of course," he warned with a cautioning wave of his index finger, "You have to realize that I'm only going to tell you the things that'll get me in your good graces."

Kevyn allowed a smile to tickle the corners of her mouth. "What makes you so sure you know the right answers?"

"I'm an expert at fielding questions from hostile reporters." He knuckled her chin up again. "You'd have to go pretty far to top them."

She angled her face away from his touch. "Perhaps we'd better sit down. This may take awhile," she remarked, grateful for any excuse to get off her trembling legs. What was she doing? she asked herself, ever aware of the man following her into the sitting room. She sank into the chaise lounge, choosing a piece of furniture that would keep him at a distance. The amused expression on his face as he took a seat on the sofa let her know he was fully aware of her purpose.

"I don't know where to start."

"I'm six-three, weigh 210—"

"You're too tall for a dancer, aren't you? I should have known better."

"You did know better, as I recall. You didn't believe me until I did a fairly credible *tour jeté*. Damn near crippled myself doing it too."

Their gazes locked. They were both remembering the same thing—not the soaring leap, but the aftermath, the steamy embrace. *Dangerous*, the voice repeated. "Your mother must have been very disappointed."

Rusty chuckled. "The second-most-asked question I ever have to answer." He crossed his long legs and leaned back, resting his head against his folded hands.

"And the first?"

"That's easy. How did a talented guy like me end up playing in the basement of the NFL?"

"Oh. Well, I guess I'm more interested in the dancing."

"How refreshing." His words held a wryly acerbic tinge. "Is my mom disappointed that I'm not a dancer? Not really. If we were in Europe, maybe she would have pushed harder. But deep down, she's as American as you or me. She's lived here for thirty years. Even that Russian blood in her veins couldn't see a practical place for a dancer with my build. Ice hockey, maybe. I was born weighing almost nine pounds. Let's face it—I'm strictly gladiator material."

Kevyn studied him, grudgingly admired his confidence. Yes, he answered questions easily and gracefully. So why did she get the feeling that there was more than he was telling? "Then why did she name you Sergei, if she didn't intend for you to be a dancer?"

He blinked, then blinked again. "That's a new question. I don't have a pat answer for that one."

"Good. I was looking for more than pat answers."

"Maybe the pat answers hold the truth." A shadow seemed to cross his face. "Or most of it. She had visions of me being an American Nureyev, possessing the best of the old world and the new. My mom had me dancing as soon as I could walk, they say. I'm sure I was poetry in motion, waddling to *Swan Lake* in diapers and a bib."

He seemed satisfied with his answer, but Kevyn wasn't. Something lurked behind that confidence, something almost pained. Remembering her own childhood, she spoke softly. "And what did your friends think about your dancing?"

"Well, let's just say it's a wonder I didn't turn into a boxer. I got a lot of practice fighting. That's why I worked so hard. I had to prove I wasn't a pansy. Nobody could run faster, jump higher, or deliver a meaner punch. Before too long, they seemed to forget I was Sergei Rivers, the 'ballerina boy.' Anyway, I quit dancing when I was about ten. By the time I got to high school I was super-jock. I lettered in everything, every year at Byrd High."

Of course, she thought. The world on a silver platter. "Were you," she said after a moment, "a good student?"

"Adequate, I guess. I damn near failed my junior year, though."

"Too much sports?"

"What is this? Twenty questions?"

She twirled a strand of hair around her fingers. "Are you uncomfortable with my asking?"

"Of course not," he said, though she felt certain he was. "But turnabout's fair play. When do I get to ask the questions?"

"Not until I'm through. About your grades—"

He gave a short laugh. "You mean almost failing my junior year?" He kneaded his knee. "It was all my mother's fault. Nobody knew how much dance I had in me, except my mother. She asked me to help this kid out, Bethany. She was my mom's pride and joy, the best pupil she ever had. Mom was grooming her for the big time. Mom was preparing her to audition in New York, and she needed a partner. Of course, I refused. Can you imagine if it had gotten back to the guys?" He seemed to focus on a distant time and place. "But then I saw her. She was a prin-

cess, tiny but strong. Blond hair, brown eyes . . .
Well, I was hooked."

"You fell in love with her."

He massaged the back of his neck. "Lord, that was
so long ago. She was fifteen years old. She had a
private tutor so she could devote her life to ballet."

"Did you help her?"

"Yeah, I helped her all right. For six months I
spent three hours a night with her and my mom—
dancing. For six months, she was all I could think
about. And in that entire time we never had a single
date, not even a conversation that wasn't centered
on dance." He chuckled at the memory. "I had her
body memorized—what there was of it. There wasn't
an inch of her that I hadn't handled, even mauled,
trying to learn those damn lifts.

"So, between athletics and dance, schoolwork
didn't have a chance. I mooched homework off of
my friends and managed to scrape by. Since I was
raised by a native speaker, my best grades were in
French . . . and they weren't that great. That spring,
we flew to New York for her audition. She won the
scholarship and was gone.

"And you know the damnedest thing?"

Kevyn waited as he stared at his fists, his auburn
brows lowering.

"That was the year the college scouts discovered
me." He met her questioning gaze. "The dancing,
the training—it was hell on my grades, but it made
me the best receiver in the state."

"What happened to her—the girl?"

"She's danced with Baryshnikov, Godunov, Mar-
tins. She got what she wanted. She's one of the
best."

Kevyn ran a finger around the rim of her empty
cup, afraid to ask the next question yet unable to
avoid it. "Do you ever see her anymore?"

"Yeah." He laughed, and the sound relieved her,
even before he explained. "I was in New York last
year for a game, and I went to see Bethany dance
with the American Ballet Theatre. Afterward, I went

back to say hello. We hugged, and she started introducing me to everyone. She was telling them how much I helped her, and you should have heard them hoot. Nobody believed her. They were on their way to a party and asked me to join them, but I couldn't. It wasn't until I was in the taxi on the way back to my hotel that I figured out what was wrong. She was so *hard*. The princess I remembered was a prima donna in every sense of the word," he said. "I love my mom, but living with one of those is enough for any man's lifetime."

Kevyn leaned her head against the back of the sofa. "I wish I could have seen you dance."

A shutter seemed to drop over his face. "I do what I do best. Isn't that enough?" His expression, the emptiness, the longing, reached out to her as no words could.

Having pushed so far, she felt a sudden need to back away quickly, before he remembered to take his own turn. "Tell me something else about you, the things you like to do, the places you like to go—besides triathlons, of course."

Rusty grimaced and held up a staying hand. "Never again. Fifty-five miles of pure unmitigated hell. Or should we call it fifty-four and a half? I didn't quite finish, did I?"

"Maybe I should have let you finish," Kevyn muttered, her cheeks coloring. "Or killed yourself trying."

"I still don't understand why you didn't."

She opened her mouth to speak, but he silenced her with a quick shake of his head.

"Now it's my turn to ask questions. I know you needed a model. I know all that. But . . ." He regarded her intently. "I keep remembering how driven, how desperate you were, and I feel like there's more going on here than just a job."

"Maybe to you a job isn't enough of an incentive. But believe me, to some people it is. I happen to need money very badly right now."

"Not to repair termite damage."

"No, no, of course not. I just—it doesn't matter.

It's taken care of now. But thank you for being concerned." An awkward silence stretched between them. Rusty leaned forward, and Kevyn felt as if she were fighting him for the very air between them.

She shot up from the chaise. "Can I get you something to drink?" She hurried past him and into the kitchen, cracking open ice trays and clattering glasses with false bravado, all in an effort to hide the shaking of her fingers.

"Having trouble?" He lounged in the doorway, his nubby cotton sweater caressing his muscled shoulders, his baggy corduroy trousers doing nothing to disguise his powerful thighs and legs from her mind's eye—that traitorous part of her that remembered their shape and texture in torturous detail.

"Here." She thrust the glass of mint tea at him and moved to push by, but his arm shot out, blocking the door.

"Do I make you nervous?" There was a teasing quality to his velvet baritone, a smooth, honeyed Louisiana drawl that sent shivers scurrying down her spine.

Bluntly, she said, "I don't think I should have let you stay."

"It didn't bother you the first time you brought me here."

"That was different, and if you don't mind, I'm really tired of discussing it."

His soft chuckle vibrated right through her. He glanced over her shoulder. "Did you know it's raining?"

She listened, and sure enough heard the soft patter of light rain hitting the large magnolia leaves and the wooden veranda. "I like rain. Especially this kind. It makes me feel shut away from the world."

His eyes narrowed. "You like being shut away?"

"I like not being bothered."

"And I'm bothering you."

"Oh, yes . . ." The words were scarcely more than a soft expulsion of breath, but they hung heavy and expectant in the air.

"Are you afraid of me?"

"Not of you." The feeling of danger skidded through her veins.

He inhaled deeply. "You feel it too?"

"I thought we'd already discussed that," she responded in a whisper.

"Yeah, and that's why I came back." His strong fingers hovered hesitantly near her face, finally brushing a strand of silver-streaked hair from her face. "It scares the hell out of me, but I'll be damned if I can leave it alone."

Kevyn's skin tingled where his callused fingertip had touched her, and her pulse throbbed violently at the base of her neck. His gaze slid over her, and she could feel its warmth like a physical caress, like fingers touching her body and testing the depths of the passion inside of her. She was as trapped by his power as if his hands held her in their grasp. Trapped by his eyes, his voice, the emotion radiating between them like an invisible bond. Trapped and tired of fighting.

With painstaking deliberation, he raised his glass to touch her lips, tilting it gently to allow the sweetened liquid to dribble into her mouth. Like a child, she swallowed. He closed her hands around the glass, cradling them between the icy-cold beverage and the roughened warmth of his skin.

Slowly, his head lowered toward hers. Slowly, he dipped closer until every inch of her body cried out for his touch.

"What are we going to do, Kevyn Llewellyn? Tell me," he whispered hoarsely. "What's the answer?"

"I don't know." She returned the glass to the counter with shaking hands.

"What is it?" he demanded softly. "Please tell me. What are we afraid of? I feel it, too, but I don't understand it."

"We're too different from each other. We're going to get hurt." She raised her face to his in an effort at defiance. She had to convince him. She had to make him see.

"Maybe, but in my business, you learn to look beyond the fear, beyond the pain, if you think the end result will be worth it. Tell me, Kevyn, is it worth it? Is it worth the risk?"

As he spoke, his hands cupped her shoulders, stroking the gauzy fabric of her blouse, moving it sensuously over her skin. Then they coasted down her arms, down the soft texture of her sleeves, until his thumbs brushed the fullness of her breasts. No amount of willpower or even fear could turn her lips away from his.

His mouth grazed hers gently, imbuing her with fear and tantalizing temptation. Her hands formed fists against the roughness of his sweater, yet her resistance melted away. A low moan sounded deep from within her throat, not really of desire, but of something more urgent, more demanding. Then his lips closed over hers, moist and warm and soft and reassuring, and she felt herself spinning under his spell. It was as if they were surrounded by an aura, an aura that protected them from the assault of doubts and fears, illuminating them and protecting them with a glimmering shield. She didn't want it to stop.

His hands slid down her body, his fingers applying firm pressure to the soft curve of her hips, pulling her against him, robbing her of all thought, leaving her victim to the sensation of his kiss, his touch, his body against hers. She was lost in him, unable to stop him, unwilling to do anything but respond. Never had she felt anything like this.

When she opened her eyes, it was to find him watching her.

Then he challenged, "Now tell me it's not worth the risk."

Six

Is it worth the risk?

Kevyn leaned against the door, gasping for breath, Rusty's voice taunting in her mind, bouncing off the recesses of forgotten memories. Though the day was cool, dewy perspiration beaded in the hollow between her breasts, and the breeze from the balcony did little to ease her torment.

He was gone. He had aroused her with his caresses, his kiss, and then, turned away and left her yearning for more. Her fingers touched her lips and lingered, searching for the heat of his kiss, then fell away to trail along the path of his touch, finally resting suggestively over her pounding heartbeat, her soft fingertips nothing like the callused ones that she'd longed to feel upon her flesh only moments before.

Thank God, he'd left.

Even after her vital signs returned to normal, her mind still reeled. He didn't know what he was offering her. He couldn't know. This attraction between them . . . yes, they both felt it, they both responded to it.

But . . . was it worth the risk?

She clenched her fists in frustration. What did he know of risks? Football? Physical risks? Physical wounds healed. Loving? She couldn't fathom him viewing loving as a risk. How many women would gladly fill the empty spaces left behind in his life by a love affair gone sour?

But, she knew, she *knew* the kind of searing pain that came when you lost someone you loved, when you were left alone. He could talk of risks. Talk was easy, too easy for him. He didn't understand.

She had already lost too much. She had learned to protect herself, for fear that one more loss would be the one to tear her in two, destroy her. Oh, yes. She *knew*.

A beckoning force drew her into the sitting room, pulling her to the low mahogany chest in the corner. She dropped to her knees and knelt before it. She took the corner of the large, hand-crocheted scarf, sweeping it away to fall unheeded to the floor. The smell of freshly stirred dust wafted up, blending with the aged scent of camphor and cedar as she raised the chest's heavy lid, its unoiled hinges creaking eerily in the musty semidarkness.

One by one, she lifted the items out, each one bringing its own wealth of memories—her father's battered pipe, still smelling of the old tobacco, or was that her heart playing tricks on her . . . her mother's faded gingham apron, once smudged with flour and cocoa and smelling of vanilla, now clean, yet wrinkled from years of being packed away.

Heath hadn't understood. He'd flown in from Atlanta, all business, pushing the attorneys, rushing the funeral director, leaving Kevyn to nurse her grief unaided.

"You don't want this old junk," he'd insisted, his dark face a study of disbelief.

She'd stood firm. She didn't care about the "valuables," much to his surprise. But she had refused to let Heath cast out those mementos of her life that lived and breathed with the essence of her beloved parents.

In a moment of weakness, she had considered returning to Atlanta with her brother. She was so lost, so alone. But each day that passed had made it more clear that any attempt to live with Heath would be disastrous. So, despite his urgings, his threats, she'd stayed in Shreveport. Being alone, even in her sorrow, had been better than being forced to live with people who didn't understand her.

If he'd known the truth about her disability, her helplessness, that she couldn't read any of his elaborate instructions, not the lawyer's name or the banker's telephone number, he never would have allowed her to stay behind. But Kevyn had already become accomplished at hiding her disability, and compensating for it in a thousand creative ways.

Eighteen years old, legally an adult, she'd put on a good front to this stranger, her brother, and sent him packing, waiting until he was gone to collapse, finally submitting to the waves of grief that engulfed her.

The belongings that were the most "worthless" held the most meaning for her: her father's pipe, her mother's apron, Rhett's ancient hi-fi. When she touched the soft, worn fabric of that apron, inhaled the sweet scent of that pipe, listened to the scratchy recordings on that record player—they lived again, if only in her memory. Heath had wanted the valuables: the war medals that heralded Rhett as a hero, the diamond wedding band that had symbolized her parents' love, old family silver. Heath had wanted those things, and she'd relinquished them without a second thought.

She needed no reminders to know that her brother had been a hero. She needed no symbols to know that her parents had loved each other. Silver tarnished; memories didn't. Her memories were rich and vivid, so vivid.

Returning the treasures to their hiding place, a sudden thought chilled her. If she opened herself up to love again, when it was over, could she cope? When all was said and done, when everything was finished, what odd tattered place of yesterday would remind her of Rusty? What scrap of seemingly worthless junk would she hide away, protect from the ravages of reality, and hoard for days like today, when the present was too threatening and only the past offered her solace?

With a sudden pang, she thought of it—a crumpled yellow swim cap, wadded into a corner of her shoulder bag, already a memento.

She closed the chest.

The following morning, she rinsed her mouth, spat mint foam into the sink, and turned off the water to hear an urgent pounding on the front door. She wrapped the black silk kimono tighter around her body and checked the tie at her waist as she hurried down the hallway.

"Who is it?" Her voice sounded tired, hoarse from a restless night, even to her own ears.

"Rusty."

His voice, his name, sent bolts of apprehension and anticipation through her. Her hand hovered over the brass knob before she finally gave in to the stronger impulse and opened the door. He looked as bad as she felt, with his face unshaven and his hair still rumpled from sleep. "It's gonna be a miserable day," he offered sheepishly.

Kevyn didn't respond. What was he doing there? And what time was it, anyway?

"I didn't mean to catch you off guard."

"That's okay," she reassured him nervously.

She hesitated, then said, "I don't usually display the social graces until after my second cup of coffee. If you want to come in, I'll be glad to make some."

"Yeah, thanks." He followed her into the kitchen and sank gratefully into a battered oak chair at the table. She was intensely aware of his presence as she moved about the outdated room, reaching for the old percolator and the coffee, freshly ground and heavily laced with chicory. Taking advantage of the fact that her back was turned to him, she surreptitiously adjusted the neckline of her robe to better cover her breasts. Then, feeling a little more secure, she took the chair opposite him.

"Remember what I said about risks?" he asked.

"Yes." The word fell between them.

"Well, it took a little scrambling, but I've got something here to help you make up your mind." He reached into the back pocket of his jeans, pulled out an envelope, and offered it to her.

"What is it?" Her fingers grasped the edge of the envelope, but he continued to hold it.

"Before you look, I want you to realize—I'm taking as big a risk as you are."

His hand fell away, and she nervously slid her finger beneath the flap and opened it. It was a ticket of some sort. She flipped it over, pretending to study it, and was rewarded for her patience.

"It's for today's game." His brows were straight, his jaw rigid. If she didn't know better, she'd think he was afraid.

"I don't understand."

"Isn't that what you don't like about me? I'm a jock, a football player. So take it. Come to the game. If it really disgusts you that much, we'll call it quits. I don't want you telling me later that you didn't understand, that you didn't know what you were getting into."

"And the risk?" she asked quietly, the coffee beginning to percolate in the background, punctuating their words.

"For you, the fact that you're admitting you're interested. Admitting that you want this as much as I do." He drummed his fingers lightly on the tabletop. "For me, two things. One, I'm exposing myself to your condescension again. I hope you realize that's not an easy thing for me. I thrive on praise, not criticism."

"And the other thing?" She watched his fingers, their tempo driving harder, vibrating the table with their heavy rhythm.

Abruptly, they stopped. He lifted his face, his eyes probing hers, his face finally softening with a smile. "We're playing the Saints. We're gonna get creamed." Seeing her pained reaction, he rushed on. "I don't mean physically. I just want you to know you're not exactly going to see me under ideal circumstances. I'm vain enough to care about things like that."

"That wouldn't make any difference to me—if I were going," she amended hastily.

"It makes a difference to me. I'm not a loser, Kevyn. I'm a fighter. Why else would I be here? Why else would I bother?" His tones grew fierce with his determination, and it almost frightened her. He had no intention of letting her go without a struggle. That was what he was telling her. Then, his mouth twisted wryly. "I had to get this ticket from a scalper. The game's been sold out for weeks."

Grasping for a noncommittal thread of conversation, she stood and crossed to the counter to pour the coffee into the small, thick, earthenware cups. "Your team must be doing very well if the tickets are that hard to come by."

"Not a chance. We haven't won a game all year. Hell, we haven't scored a touchdown yet."

"Then why—"

"Why'd the game sell out? Because it's *New Orleans*. There were two games that we knew would draw crowds—Dallas and New Orleans. Shreveport's full of Cowboy and Saint fans. They've been pretty loyal at the other games, even if the stadium wasn't filled. But against the Saints?" He rubbed the back of his neck. "It won't take much for the fans to start rooting for them. After all, they've been Louisiana's only pro team for a long time. We're the new kids on the block. I don't want to think about Dallas. With Texas Stadium only three hours west on I20, lots of Shreveport natives never miss a Cowboy game."

Kevyn set a steaming mug of rich-scented coffee in front of him. "And your knee?"

"So-so. That's why I've got to get there early. I've got to get taped up and ready for battle." Tilting the cup to his lips, he gulped it down. "In fact, I'm late already. That'll probably be a two hundred dollar fine. Coach'll be on the lookout for everybody today."

"Two hundred dollars?"

He stood up and stretched. "Yeah, that's pretty standard. The only way to keep us animals in line is to get us where it hurts—the paycheck. But, don't worry. The coffee was worth it. Damn good coffee." Gone was the brooding hostility, the warrior preparing for battle. "Besides, I don't want the old guy to think he's got me running scared. A little assertive independence is more my style."

"I never doubted it for a minute."

"So you'll be there?"

"I don't know." He was pushing her too fast, too hard. She needed time to think.

"The seat isn't that good—it's on the twenty-yard line and pretty high up—but it was the best I could do on such short notice." He touched a strand of her hair, rubbing its texture between his rough fingertips.

"Rusty," she whispered as his fingers brushed against her cheek. "I don't know. I can't make any promises."

His hand skimmed down her cheek to her jawline, his knuckles rasping gently along its contours before sliding down her neck to linger longingly at the neckline of her robe. His eyes peered deeply into hers, no longer challenging, only beseeching. As his fingers caressed her collarbone, he said, "Please. Give us a chance."

"Why are you pushing me like this? What do you want from me?"

"That's the hell of it. I don't know yet. But I intend to find out." Raising his hand in a slight gesture of repentance, he shook his head silently.

As she heard the front door close behind him, she leaned forward over the counter, resting her forehead on one of the cool, glass-paned cabinet doors. Why did he have to push her to make a decision now? Why the ticket? Wasn't there some other way?

Rusty sat on the padded vinyl table, wincing as

Ernie prodded and rotated his knee. "Dammit, take it easy!"

"Touchy today, ain't ya'," the trainer drawled, his face contorted in a thoughtful scowl. He stuck a stubby finger under the joint of Rusty's knee and probed. Rusty jerked away, and the older man's heavy eyebrows lowered ominously. "Are you gonna need some novocaine?"

"No, no needles." He was relieved when the older man released him, handing him a foam sleeve to wear on his knee. Rusty grimaced and waved it away. "I'm not wearing that thing—it just slows me down."

"Yeah, yeah, yeah. Just don't come whinin' to me when—"

Rusty retreated toward his locker, not waiting to hear the rest of the threat. Piece by piece, he pulled on his equipment, all marked with his number, 86. When he'd tugged his gray game pants over his armor-like equipment—shin guards, knee pads, thigh pads, hip pads—he bounced lightly on his toes, checking his mobility. A voice from behind halted him as he reached for his jersey.

"Hey, Rivers. Gonna catch any today?"

He stiffened, closing his fingers on the gold jersey, and faced Dirk Weaver, the talented rookie wide receiver who was hovering behind him on the second string, waiting like a vulture for his opportunity to prove his superiority to Rusty and become a starter. Forcing his tone to be casual, Rusty answered, "Sure. Are you?" He pulled the shirt over his head.

"Yeah, you know me, I'm always ready to catch a few. Just wondered if *you'd* be up to it, though, after all your carousin' Friday night. Saw you in the paper—nice picture. It captured the real you." Weaver propped one foot on the bench and leaned his elbow on his heavily padded thigh. "Good-lookin' lady too."

A slow red haze threatened to obscure Rusty's vision. It wasn't bad enough that he had to fight this guy for his position—now he was supposed to put up with his smart-ass comments as well? He turned his back on the blond wide receiver and grabbed his helmet.

Then, facing Weaver eye to eye, he allowed a patronizing tone to enter his voice. "I don't intend to miss any catches today, or next week, or the week after that. So, if you're trying to rattle me on that account, you can get those wild ideas right out of your head."

Weaver seemed amused, but his voice contained a thinly veiled threat. "I don't have to have any 'wild ideas' about your job, Rivers. Everybody knows you're washed up. The Colonel just wanted you for publicity—hometown boy on the hometown team. After this year, you're gone." He emphasized his last point by slamming his fist into his hand, then laughed maliciously. "Take care of that knee, buddy. One wrong step, and you won't last the year."

Rusty looked into the younger man's face and saw yesterday . . . his own cockiness, arrogance, world-by-a-string confidence. He felt old, and it had nothing to do with aching joints or candles on a cake. "We've got a game to play, Weaver. Save your energy for that, and remember this one thing if you don't remember anything else—losers take potshots at their own teammates. Winners don't have to."

The lanky young receiver snorted, then walked away.

Rusty sank onto the bench, relieved when the kid was gone. But he felt anything but calm. He tightened his fingers into fists and dropped his head and closed his eyes, fighting to still the turmoil that raged within him. Weaver hadn't said anything that hadn't been said before, or that hadn't been written in the papers, for that matter. Rusty could hide his feelings from Weaver, but he couldn't hide from the truth—that somehow he'd let his career slip through his fingers.

The Gents weren't Rusty's last chance to make

good—he'd wasted those chances. This was his last hurrah.

Rusty's head snapped up. Kevyn. Had she come? The thought of her slanting blue eyes watching him left him disoriented, agitated. Why had he given her that damned ticket?

She had him so confused. She somehow seemed to be as beautiful and protected as an exquisite watercolor behind glass, as warm and soothing as a whirlpool, and as maddening as crosstown traffic, all at the same time. So why did he feel the perilous urge to smash the glass, spill the water, and damn the madness?

"You must be a Saints fan." The gray-haired gentleman on Kevyn's left held out a Styrofoam cup of steaming coffee. Indicating his large thermos, he added, "I've got plenty, and you look like you could use some."

She hesitated, then accepted it gratefully, cupping the warm cup in her hands. "Yes, please. I had no idea it would be so cold. It didn't seem this bad at home."

"First game here, eh? I can tell. Anybody who's been here before knows about the windchill. Next time you'll know better."

Kevyn nodded numbly. Next time? That was a disquieting thought. She'd sat quietly through the first three quarters, not understanding a thing that was happening down on the field.

The scoreboard offered more entertainment than the game, with its flashing lights and cartoon characters and instant-replay screens. Not that she could read the score—but the Gents hadn't scored a single point, so she supposed the exact score of the Saints wasn't that important in the long run. The players seemed unreal, like matchstick figures in some bizarre choreographed dance, bouncing off each other and rolling over each other, and accomplishing little. Only the halftime activities had made any sense at all, with marching bands, dancing girls, and even a dog-and-Frisbee competition. Halftime had been too brief as far as she was concerned. After sipping the coffee, she looked at her neighbor. "Why did you think I was a Saints fan?"

He glanced at her sweater, surprised. "You're wearing Saints colors. That's usually a pretty good indicator of which way your loyalties lie."

Kevyn eyed her wool sweater, a black knobby-knit with metallic gold threads shot through it. Worn with black wool slacks, it was the warmest casual outfit she had. Then she looked back at the field, and the team in black. "Saints colors? I didn't realize . . ." She experienced a sinking feeling, which was quickly submerged in nervous panic. What if Rusty saw her? What on earth would he think?

"Then you're rooting for the Gents?" the elderly man asked. "Come to think of it, you've been mighty quiet. Are you rooting for anybody?"

"Not exactly . . ." Except for Rusty, she amended silently. She was rooting for him. The rest made no difference.

As the players lined up for the start of the fourth quarter, she studied them. He wasn't out there this time. It was so confusing—sometimes he was playing, and sometimes he wasn't. Just when she got used to watching the ball go one way, they stopped everything and started over in the other direction.

She'd only seen Rusty catch the ball three times, and each time someone had knocked him down before he could run with it. She shook her head in amazement. This was what meant so much to him? Submerged in her own thoughts, she sat lost to the actions on the field and oblivious to the reactions of the crowd around her.

Then, she caught sight of him again. Pacing the sidelines, his helmet under his arms, she felt the familiar stirring in her breast. With his carriage, sleek and powerful, his hair, gleaming in the slanting rays of the afternoon sun, *he* wasn't a match-stick figure. Her pulse quickened in response.

Even from across a crowded stadium, the sight of him reached out and grabbed her, twining its way into her imagination, her thoughts. She felt a melting glow, a glow that spread throughout her body with tenacious thoroughness. And with it, a fierce possessiveness. That man wanted her, just as she was trying not to want him. He even . . . dare she think it? . . . needed her. Just as she so desperately was trying not to need him.

The crowd was on its feet, and suddenly, she joined them. What was happening? Rusty was pulling on his helmet. He ran out on the field with two other players, their paths intersecting those of three players heading for the sidelines. The Gents, the team in gray and gold, *his* team, were lined up closer to the end of the field than they had been all day. That had to be good, she thought. Sensing the enthusiasm in the crowd, she knew it *was* good. Of course it was good—Rusty was out there. She felt the excitement building, the anticipation as he bent over, his fingertips touching the turf, his head raised and turned toward the center. The crowd quieted for just a moment, then at the snap roared to life again.

Unable and unwilling to follow any other action on the field, Kevyn's eyes remained fixed on Rusty. He ran as fleet-footed as any jungle animal, then cut sharply to the left, deftly evaded a pursuer in black and gold, and suddenly, almost in slow motion, sprung into the air, flying higher, higher. His arms stretched out over his head, his hands reaching . . . reaching . . . then closing around the football that seemed to appear miraculously at the precise moment needed.

Then, a second pair of hands snatched the ball from Rusty's grasp. The crowd's screaming, groaning reaction reverberated through the stadium. Landing easily, the player in black instantly turned and headed in the opposite direction, up the field.

Kevyn ignored the ensuing chase, the interception

that turned into a touchdown. Her eyes were riveted to Rusty as he fell to the turf empty-handed. He landed on his knee and crumpled to the ground.

Why wasn't he getting up? Why wasn't he moving?

A man came off the sidelines and knelt beside him, then another joined the first, until Rusty was surrounded by men in street clothes instead of uniforms. Doctors? Trainers? Unaware that her fingernails were biting into her tender palms until she felt the moist blood under them, Kevyn watched desperately as they surrounded him.

Why wasn't he getting up?

Then, she saw his arm sweep out, waving them away. Oh, how she remembered that gesture, that defiant, determined gesture. It was as if she were down there with them. *I'm doin' fine. . . . Leave me alone. . . . I don't need any help. . . .*

She wasn't surprised when he rose shakily and refused assistance. As he limped from the field, Kevyn sank back to her seat, able to breathe again. She stared down at her hands, palms marked with half-moons of red. *This* was what he loved. *This*— could she really call it a game?—was what she had to share him with.

Suddenly, she couldn't watch anymore. She rose unsteadily and began pushing down the row to the aisle. Clutching her leather shoulder bag tightly to her side, she wedged her way through the mob in the aisle. She cast one last look over her shoulder.

She didn't see him at first, but then, standing off by himself, she saw his unmistakable form. He stood erect, his shoulders impossibly wide under the gold jersey and pads, his hips impossibly slim in comparison, his gray and gold helmet under his arm. Then, he turned his head, angling it toward her. But there was no way he could see her. No way he could pick her out in the crowd. Yet, she felt his eyes scanning, searching. Did he know? Could he feel her presence?

And drawing a steadying breath, she realized the truth. For whatever reason, he *was* looking for her.

He needed her. He wanted her to be something she didn't know how to be. . . .

People pushed around her as she stood her ground against the flow of movement. First slowly, then with more determination, she began forcing her way against the crowd, fighting her way back to her seat.

Despite her uncertainty, she felt compelled to stay.

Please, he had said. *Give me a chance.*

A chance at what? What did he want from her, she who had nothing to give to someone like him? Kevyn moved restlessly, lighting candle after candle until her bedroom was incandescent with a flickering glow.

She heard a low rumble of thunder in the distance and went to the studio to check the doors and windows. Picking her way carefully between easels and tables, she moved through the darkness to close a set of French doors. She didn't want to flood the room with light, to expose the canvases, the sketches, and what was beginning to feel like the emptiness of her life. Funny, it hadn't seemed empty before. Not until a certain warrior-god, a dancing Russian prince had . . . had what? Had tantalized her with the promise of things that could not come. A chill of apprehension rippled down her spine.

She reached for the French doors, her fingers on the old lock that was prone to stick at the best of times and that tonight seemed more obstinate than usual. Light flashed, leaving the old magnolia's black silhouette imprinted on her eyes. Uneasiness stirred within her, a need she couldn't name, and suddenly, rather than securing the lock, she flung open the doors and stepped onto the balcony. Again, thunder rumbled, closer, louder, and a restless energy stirred within her. She filled her lungs with the crisp night air and tasted the moisture of the impending storm. As she crossed to the rail, her pulse quickened. The wind whipped around her; it caught at her robe and billowed it behind her; it sent dry leaves skittering around her bare feet.

Then she saw headlights sweep the road and turn into the oak-shrouded gravel driveway. They sliced across her, blinding her. It was several moments before she could see across the yard. Startled, she clasped her robe at the neck and whirled to run back inside, but above the sound of wind and leaves and creaking boughs, she recognized the low purr of a sports car, and she stopped, poised between flight and expectancy. Then the car stopped. In silence, she watched. As the first drops of rain began to fall, Rusty dashed across the lawn.

A jagged bolt of lightning split the sky, and she was shaken by the image it captured. In that single frame of time she saw his grace, his speed, his power. One split second of frozen motion, but it was etched on her mind with the vivid detail of a photograph. Had he seen her standing on the balcony? She pulled the black satin robe tightly around her, closed the neckline with nervous fingers, and edged back to the gaping glass doors of the studio. Despite the sound of the rapidly increasing downpour, she heard him coming up the stairs. And she stayed. Poised in the doorway, she waited.

He appeared at the corner of the balcony, his hair sprinkled with droplets of rain, and seeing her, he slowed his pace. Another bolt of lightning, and another memory of high cheekbones, beautiful lips, and heavily lashed eyes was imprinted on her mind— another picture to tuck away, to pore over in solitude.

"You shouldn't have come."

"I'll leave if you want me to."

A gust of wind blew the rain onto the balcony, and they were showered with its sparkling moisture, yet neither of them flinched or wavered. The elements crashed around them. Something stronger, more elemental, hovered between them.

Unless she moved away now, at once, she would fall in and drown. What an insane notion, yet that was what she felt—a drowning, choking, frightening desire that filled her with the scents, the tastes, of foolish, forbidden longings.

Then, with a seductively innocent movement, Rusty touched her, and the fragile plane of caution between them shattered. She couldn't tear her gaze away from his rain-glazed features as he slowly, wondrously, cupped her face. She felt his thumb drag across her cheek and down her neck, and she shivered. Then his lips followed that same trail, and she trembled. Finally, with his breath, his lips, his wordless whispers rustling in the soft hollow at the base of her throat, she felt the waters closing over her head.

A soft whimper, her own, sounded in the night. *Touch me, please touch me.* Had she really spoken those words, or was it merely the wind? No matter . . . he heard, he understood.

He kissed her.

Then his lips left hers, trailing down her neck, leaving a scattering of sparks in their wake as his fingers spread the neck of her robe open and exposed her flesh to the chill of the night, to the heat of his kiss.

Still he continued, with his hands gathering the black silk of her kimono in greedy handfuls, bunching it until the hem skimmed up her thighs, until his fingers found the bare flesh of her derriere and pressed into her with savage insistence.

He raised his eyes to hers, his pupils large and dark with passion. Then, he pulled away. Leaving her craving his touch, he slowly glided his hands down her thighs, dragging the moment out as if the thought of not touching her was more than he could bear.

When he spoke, his voice was heavy and rasping, his breathing as labored as her own. "I mean it, Kevyn. I want you to understand what you're getting into. I am what I am, nothing more, nothing less. If that's not enough for you . . . stop me now."

Enough . . . what was enough? He was robbing

her of reason, was blinding her to sense, was taking her will to resist and turning it to dust. Suddenly, surely, she knew that whatever he had to give her, if for only this night, was not only enough, it was necessary to her ability to live, to feel, to soar.

It was so easy to give in, so easy to let go. She tilted her head back, her lips parting. Never mind tomorrow. Never mind misgivings. This was tonight. This was what she wanted.

"Touch me," she whispered, and this time there was no doubting that the words were spoken. This time he lifted her into his arms. So easily, so effortlessly, he cradled her, one arm circling under her back and shoulders, the other circling over and behind her knees . . . so, so strong . . . and she felt a strange comfort there.

"Where?" he asked hoarsely.

"Down the hall, last room on the left."

She leaned against him, giving in to the smooth rocking motions as he carried her. Her hands wandered at will, exploring the smooth, hard contours of his shoulders beneath his damp sweater, and her concept of the male body changed. She was no longer content to look, to sketch, to re-create; she wanted to feel his masculine perfection against her, the smoothness of his skin and the strength of his body, with her palms, her lips, her body.

Then he stopped, and she watched his face, glowing with the flickering warmth of a dozen candles, as his lips parted in wonder. "What is this place?"

"This is where I dream."

A dream.

He had come there bruised and battered, thirsting for a solace he didn't understand, and somehow, he had stumbled into a dream.

He stood in the doorway of her bedroom, her weight in his arms warming, stirring, the dull throb of his muscles muted, almost forgotten, and felt as if he were stepping from the dusty, crowded wings backstage into a strangely lit backdrop of candle-lit fantasy.

The walls were dark blue, just shades away from purple or black, almost undulating in the flickering light of two dozen candles. On the far wall a silvery Pegasus winged across the night sky, shimmering with the light of iridescent moonbeams, wings outspread in wide, glorious abandon.

This is where I dream.

He looked down at Kevyn, her body suddenly tense in his arms, and he realized she was staring at him, watching him with eyes dark and black and shadowed, as if she were waiting. Waiting for him to . . . to what? Why did he feel that if he moved wrong, if he breathed wrong, she would dissolve, would disappear? He felt as if he were playing a game where he didn't know the rules. A game that if lost, would leave him with a gaping emptiness where he'd once been strong and whole.

He didn't know what was happening, he only knew that suddenly he wanted nothing more than to capture those lips, to taste them. He bent his head to hers, and she didn't dissolve—she melted against him. He kissed her lips, her cheek, her chin, each movement more fierce, more frantic as he sought something he couldn't define. Her fingers fluttered against his throat, his ears, finally closed around the back of his neck and pulled him closer, harder, with a desperation he could taste. He could hardly breathe for the agony, the crazy, crazy agony of what he was feeling. He broke away and drew in a deep, shuddering breath and met her eyes, dark pools of confusion and desire and need . . . why? Why the intensity that seemed almost pain? Pain that he felt closing around his own heart as it pounded against hers, faster and harder, feeding off her emotion. *Slow down—slow down,* a voice warned.

His right arm supporting her back, his left circling her knees, he stood, chest heaving, and fought for control. Too fast. Things were moving too fast.

Slowly he shifted her weight and released her knees, sliding his hand up her thighs to her waist, easing her legs down until she had rotated to face him. So slowly, so gently, so erotically her body slid against his as he lowered her until her toes touched the floor, a move that came as naturally to him as if he even now stood in his mother's studio—and he felt a strange, panicky kind of laughter building in his throat.

He was holding her the way a dancer would.

Jarred by the thought, he dropped his arms.

She didn't seem to notice. Toe, ball, heel, she settled to the floor, and then glanced over her shoulder to the only furniture in the room, a vast sleigh bed of black mahogany, covered with white—white quilts, pillows, and mosquito netting that spun downward from a hoop mounted high on the ceiling. She pivoted and glided toward it, glancing back at him once, as she loosened the knot at her waist. Images of her portrait, filmy gossamer and jeweled tones, sped through his mind, only to be quickly dismissed. This was real. She was real, and he was so filled with the warmth of her, the taste of her, the touch of her . . . he knew no need but one—to bury himself inside her.

He crossed the distance between them without thinking, and when she would have removed her robe he swept her hands away. The silk kimono no longer hugged her waist, but now hung loosely, giving whisper glimpses of the milk-white skin only a lover would see. He slid his hands over her shoulders, tunneling under the soft fabric, easing it open bit by bit. The satin slid down but caught on her breasts, and her lips parted and she shuddered as he slipped his hands down the soft swells, slowly, slowly skimmed his fingers lower, until they danced across the peaks and freed them. She gasped at his touch, yet strained toward it. Her shudder radiated through her body, and his arms closed about her, pulling her more tightly against him. He cupped her breast, felt her heart pounding, her nipple hardening against his palm, and suddenly had to possess that perfect breast, to taste it, to make her writhe against him, to stir a passion of his own making in those slanting eyes, a passion and emotion that didn't confuse him, one that he could understand.

He used no gentleness as his lips found her dusky rose nipples. His movements seemed to take on the rhythm of the blood pulsing through his veins as he suckled her sweet flesh and felt her swell, tighten as he pulled soft whimpering moans from deep in her throat. He sank to his good knee and kneaded her soft buttocks with his strong fingers, sliding the silky kimono over her curves, sliding, squeezing, until he couldn't think or breathe or even exist, except to touch her. Then, in a desperate, frantic motion, she wrenched herself away from him and he knew a moment of panic.

She arched her neck, her back, and the robe slid to the floor . . . and he stared.

Lit by flickering candlelight, framed by midnight, she was a sprite come to torment him, to tantalize him, to fulfill his raging need. From the shimmering halo of wild, tangled hair to the eyes that darkened with a need he shared, a pain he feared, a haunting that bewildered and frightened him; from the delicate shoulders to the swollen breasts that gleamed with wetness from his own kiss; from the flaring hips to the long, slender legs that tensed and flexed and quivered at his touch . . . she stood before him, bathed in gold and shadows, offering him so much. Yet, somehow, he knew that behind that need and haunting pain, she was hiding far more. . . .

"Please . . ." she whispered. "Hold me . . . hold me."

As he gazed into her face the immensity of her need distended his flesh, the knowledge of her pain engulfed his heart—why couldn't he wipe it away? Why, when her eyes were dilated with a passion of his creation, couldn't he make the pain disappear? He couldn't swallow, couldn't move, couldn't think. His breath shuddered in his chest as the desire to be slow and gentle and the need to possess warred within him.

She dipped to her knees, knelt before him, and took his face in her hands. The lips that closed over his tasted of sweet desire, of sweet hunger. The hands that groped at his waist, his belt, trembled. His hunger surged. He pulled his sweater over his head and flung it to the floor, strained and tugged at his pants, his briefs, his shoes, until there was nothing separating them but damp night air. He pulled her up with him and dropped to the edge of the bed, and as she came to him and pressed against him, his gaze raised to the midnight mural on the wall. *Where I dream,* she had said. His fingers trailing through the veil of her hair, Rusty felt the tendrils of tension sneaking back into him. That picture—who had painted it? Kevyn? Or Simon Killingsworth? Something very male in him reacted to the thought and the fear that the haunted look in her eyes was the shadow of another man.

"Touch me," he said, when he really meant, *What am I, who am I to you?* But when she reached and found him and stroked him and closed her hand around him, he buried his face in her neck, in her hair, and groaned as all thought fled but the exquisite pain. He pressed his hand between her thighs and found her wet and burning for him, quivering at his touch as he slid a finger in, out, in, out, until she twisted and writhed in his arms, danced to a rhythm of *his* making, a fire of *his* stoking, a need that *he* would fill—no one else. She choked out his name, *his* name, and he knew not triumph, but relief.

He stretched over her, pushing her onto the bed, covering her with his body, and as she arched wildly toward him, he rubbed her heat, her wetness, and allowed her to guide him in. The blood roared in his veins as she sheathed him, pulsed around him, and she gasped as he began moving with a primitive rhythm that sprang from deep within him, sensitive flesh stroking sensitive flesh, a dance as old as the

"I'm making a memory."

"You're beautiful . . . so beautiful." He tangled his fingers in the ebony and lace of her hair, and pulled her closer to touch his lips to hers.

She nestled against him. "What are you thinking?"

He seemed to struggle with his thoughts, and when he spoke, his voice was hoarse and strange. "All I know is that when I'm with you, I feel like anything can happen—any crazy, ridiculous, wonderful thing. It's like you're surrounded with it, an aura, a halo. I don't know what it is, but I know that right now, at this moment, I want it never to end . . ." His lips traced the delicate curve of her collarbone with feather-light pressure, and his words brushed across her skin as warm puffs of air.

"Nothing lasts, Rusty." She rested her cheek on the top of his head. "Nothing."

He didn't answer at first. Then, he simply responded with another kiss, this one on her mouth, a kiss that drained her and filled her, and removed all never-ending, nothing-lasting thoughts from her mind, from her soul.

Pain seeped into Rusty's body, exhaustion and pain. He needed to rest, if just for a while. He propped himself against the pillow-cushioned back of the sleigh bed and looked down at Kevyn, cradled in his arms.

Of course, nothing lasted. That was understood. His life was filled with only one certainty: Don't count on anything. But he didn't want to think about that. He didn't want to think about the jangling alarm in his head, or the coach who expected him to call, or any of a multitude of thoughts that normally filled his mind. For now, for this moment in time, he felt a mystical wonder that not even the ominous words "Nothing lasts" could dispel.

His fingers tangling through her hair, Rusty considered the midnight mural on the wall. "You painted that, didn't you?"

"Why?"

How could he tell her that the thought of her dreaming under the outspread wings of Simon Killingsworth's Pegasus had eaten at him, frustrated him, until he realized that the painting was hers, not Simon's. It was her magic that touched the horse's eyes with liquid gentleness, yet showed tense muscles rippling under a coat of ivory hair. Pegasus, soaring into the night sky, seeking . . . always seeking. Finally, simply, he said, "It's beautiful."

He had to ask. He hated himself for caring, but he had to ask. He raised up on one elbow, trailing his fingers down her side. Hadn't he given her a piece of him when he had told her about Bethany, about his dancing—things he had never shared before? So, probing the depths of her shadows and risking the strengthening of her walls, he asked, "How did you end up with Killingsworth?"

He felt her tension. He touched her shoulder; she flinched and lay back in the circle of his arm, averting her gaze from his. "I loved him, that's all. We loved each other . . . for a while."

Nothing lasts . . .

"I owe him a great deal. He saved me."

"From what?" His throat tightened, and his voice was gruffer than intended.

"From being lost. From being alone." She rolled over and lay on her stomach, her cheek resting on her folded hands, watching him through those cloudy eyes. "After my parents died . . . I was very alone, very frightened, very hurt. I . . . needed help. Miss Lucy asked Simon to look at my art, which he said was dreadful but showed promise, and . . . well, he always said he took me in like a lost bird." Her low laughter echoed in the still room. "Simon got me my first illustration work."

Her words echoed in his head: *He saved me. . . . I needed help.* Again, he found himself playing a game, pitted against a foe, where he didn't know the rules, didn't know the enemy. Again, he felt that if he pushed too hard, asked too much, she would coil away from him and close him out. Yet he couldn't stop one last question. "Were you lovers?"

"Not at first. Not for a long time. But, finally . . . yes. He was older, and that worried him a lot. Even later, he sometimes looked . . . sad. He knew what I didn't—that it would never work. We were too much alike." No strain, no tension here. He searched her face for the pain and found none, and was relieved yet confused. She tugged a long tendril of hair, twisted it dreamily between her fingers. "That's why he could help me, and why when I was strong enough, I could let him go." Her voice lowered to a whisper. "Like I said, nothing lasts forever."

So you make memories.

He stared at the soaring, seeking Pegasus. "Sometimes . . . don't you ever think that maybe there *is* something just out of reach, something that lasts, if only you could touch it, and hold it, and . . ." He didn't know how to finish, what to say. His nervous laughter filled the air. "Oh, hell. Listen to me, sounding like a damn poet. Is that what hanging around you does to a man?"

"Is that so bad?"

"Maybe not . . . maybe that's what scares me."

"Rusty," she whispered, "love me again."

Later, much later, the whirring and grinding of the dumbwaiter roused Kevyn from her sleep. Instantly awake, she slipped on her robe and ran into the hallway to find Miss Lucy's limp body curled into the small enclosure, her eyes glassy and frightened.

"I'm so sorry, dear . . ." Her voice was little more than the rustling of brittle leaves, a soft rasp.

Kevyn pressed a hand against Miss Lucy's forehead. Her skin felt papery dry and hot. "Rusty! Help me, quick!" The words tore from her throat as the old woman slumped sideways into her arms. Kevyn realized she was so slight, so birdlike, that she could have carried her herself.

But Rusty was at her side, pulling his trousers over his slim hips. "What happened?"

"She's burning up with fever." She looked up at him over Miss Lucy's limp body, and his face wavered in her sight—her face was wet—she was crying. "Rusty, help her."

He lifted the woman's frail body and carried her down the hall. Kevyn dashed ahead of him, smoothed the rumpled bedclothes, and covered them with a fresh quilt. Her arms clutching her middle, she watched Rusty lower the elderly woman ever so gently to the bed.

His brow creased with concern. "I think you'd better call the doctor, Kevyn."

". . . too much trouble . . . I'm sorry . . ." the old woman rasped, appearing startled when she saw Rusty towering over her. She tossed her head sideways. "Kevyn? Kevyn?"

Kevyn quickly shushed her. Fighting down the lump of terror in her chest, she met Rusty's gaze across the expanse of the bed. "Call an ambulance," he said.

She couldn't stop shivering.

The hospital corridor was so cold, so frightening. Even with Rusty's jacket around her shoulders, his arm around her, Kevyn shuddered with the cold.

"What time is it?" she asked.

Rusty checked the clock high on the wall. "Four-fifteen. They've been working on her for almost two hours." He dragged his free hand through the rumpled waves of his hair. "Why don't you let me call my dad? He's on staff here. He can make some phone calls and get some action—"

The double doors swung open and the young resident on duty pushed through. "Miss Llewellyn?"

Kevyn jumped to her feet. Rusty rose beside her.

"Mrs. Perkins has a relatively mild infection along

with her virus," the doctor said. "But at her age even a mild infection can be serious. We're going to give her some intravenous fluids, try to bring down her fever."

"She doesn't want to stay here," Kevyn said. "She wants to go home."

"Is there anyone who can take care of her? I'm talking round-the-clock care, someone who you can depend on."

Kevyn raised her chin. "Of course there is. I will."

The resident considered her for a moment. "That's totally up to you, of course. I'd suggest you wait until morning to take her home, though. She's already had a rough night." Then he appeared to soften. "In fact, you look like you have too. Why don't you go on home and get some rest? You may not get much for the next couple of days."

"He's right, Kevyn," Rusty said. "If you're going to do this, you'd better go home and get some sleep."

Her shoulders ached with weariness, her eyes felt gritty, and she didn't dare consider what a tangled mess her hair was. His arm around her shoulders felt so good. It would be so easy to grow accustomed to his strength, to having someone to lean on.

"No," she said. "I'll stay with her. You go home and sleep. I don't want to be responsible for you getting in trouble with your coach again." She gave Rusty back his jacket, and tried to pretend that the world didn't suddenly seem a few degrees colder.

For three days she cared for Miss Lucy; for three days she slept and ate downstairs and was only in her own studio for a few hours a day; for two more days she continued to use Miss Lucy's illness as an excuse not to see Rusty when he made his daily telephone call. By Friday, Miss Lucy had improved enough to be left alone at night. Kevyn slept in her own bed again, remembering her last night there. Now that there were no excuses, she wondered if she would have the strength to tell him no again, when he called again.

On Saturday he didn't call.

The hours stretched long and lonely before she remembered—

Rusty was on a chartered plane for Washington.

With him out of reach, out of touch, it was so much easier to convince herself that she was relieved.

The four walls were closing in on him.

Rusty stood in the center of the room, a myriad of emotions sweeping through him. How many curfews in how many hotel rooms in how many cities had he endured? They ran together in a blur, one melting into the next in his memory.

But this wasn't just any hotel room or just any road trip.

This was Washington, D.C.

Downstairs, a platoon of sportswriters was waiting with acerbic pens. Catching sight of himself in the mirror, he saw an expression of wry condemnation twisting his features. "Welcome home, buddy." And one hell of a homecoming party was waiting for him, with over sixty thousand fans in RFK Stadium. This time, however, they wouldn't be screaming for him. He was on the wrong team.

Seven years before, it had been where his pro career had started. He'd flown into town, a top draft pick with a big contract and high expectations, only to be traded four years later—a failure.

Staring into the mirror, he saw eyes that had once glittered with the challenge of the game, now lined with anxiety and frustration. His knee throbbed, his stomach was knotted with tension. Where was the Redskins' golden boy now? A low mirthless chuckle came from his throat, and in a savage gesture he peeled his shirt over his head and flung it across the room.

"What happened?" he demanded, baring his body to the brutal honesty of the mirror's reflection. His muscles were tensed and ropelike over his shoulders, his stomach smooth and flat, tapering to the place where the faint vee of hair disappeared beneath his jeans. "What happened?" he repeated viciously, his fists clenched as if ready to fight the stranger with the taunting eyes.

And then, he caught the mocking gleam in the mirror image, the flashing reflection of the ring—the Super Bowl ring he'd earned his last season—here, earned by sitting on the bench in a strike-torn season, short by NFL standards, yet the longest season of his career due to the trade rumors flying. It was with a surge of savagery that he saw the reflection come to life, swinging up at him until its fist met his, slamming together ring to ring in a shattering of glass that sent splintered fragments in all directions. Mercifully, the image was gone. He stared hollow-eyed and panting at the blank wall, at the broken shards of mirror, and then, down at his hand. Transfixed, he raised his still-clenched fist, his gaze centering on the long shallow cuts barely discernible from the other wrinkles on his knuckles. And then the blood came, trickling down his arm and dripping gently on the beige carpet. So much blood from such a little wound . . . he walked hypnotically into the bathroom, splashed icy water over his hand, wrapped a towel around it, and sunk slowly to the floor.

Minutes dragged by, shadows lengthening, the sun setting, darkness spreading its murky fingers into the room. He heard knocking on the door, Skipper's call, and the voices receding when he didn't respond. It just didn't seem to matter anymore. They'd be talking about the game, laughing, joking to cover their frustration, and tossing around hopeless "what ifs." Because there was no doubt in anyone's mind what would happen—the Gents didn't stand a chance. And for the first time, Rusty admitted to himself he didn't care. His career was over. His tailspin was about to come to a crashing conclusion . . . and he just didn't care anymore.

When the phone rang again, this time piercing through the fog of his self-pity, he could think of a dozen people it might be—but he knew it wouldn't be the one voice he needed to hear. Suddenly, he jerked to his feet and lunged for the telephone. His hand hovered above it as he waited for it to stop ringing. Finally, it did.

Quickly he reached for the receiver and put it to his ear, blurting out the number to the operator. Waiting anxiously for the call to go through, he counted the rings—three, six . . . too many. She wasn't there. Still he waited, his fingers clutching the telephone with desperation until . . . she answered.

"Kevyn?"

"Rusty? Is that you?"

She sounded good, so damned real. "Yeah, it's me. What are you doing?" he asked, struggling for a steady tone.

"I'm working on some sketches. Rusty, aren't you supposed to be in Washington?"

"Yeah, I'm here. . . . You should see the view—it's great, if you like rain." His eye fixed dazedly on the closed draperies spanning one wall of the room. "I can barely make out the Washington Monument. Have you ever seen it?"

"No, I haven't. . . . Rusty, are you sure you're all right?"

She sounded anxious, and it felt so damn good to think that she really cared.

"I mean," she continued, "you didn't call to tell me about the view, did you?"

"Not really. I just . . ." He inhaled deeply. "I just wanted to hear your voice." He grimaced in reaction to his own words, grateful that she couldn't see the ruddy color staining his cheeks. Lord, he sounded like a love-struck kid. "And check on Miss Lucy," he added in a rush.

"She's still very weak. I'll tell her you were concerned enough to call. And she loves your flowers."

Her gentle tone unnerved him. "Yeah," he said,

the tension easing out of his shoulders. "Do that. . . . And you sound great."

"You . . . you sound good too."

He pictured the way she was probably brushing her hair away from her face, and the image soothed him. But then his gaze fell on the bloodstained towel wrapped around his fist. Seeing it, he immediately felt the throbbing pain.

"Uh, Kevyn, I really need to go now. I have to take care of some things before curfew."

"All right," she answered softly. "I hope your game goes well."

"I feel pretty good about it," he said, and suddenly realized he was telling the truth. After their good-byes he returned the receiver to its cradle. He straightened slowly, flexing his bad knee. It felt solid, and remarkably, he felt good, strong. Ready to start over again—even in D.C.

The flight had been hell; they had hit turbulence over the Appalachians that hadn't settled until just before landing in Shreveport. But to Rusty the ride had been smooth as silk, coming off a great game, a *great* game, against the Redskins.

But now, driving ten miles over the speed limit on the winding asphalt road, he had only one goal—Kevyn. He turned into the driveway and cut the motor. He eased out of the car and shut the door quietly, unable to suppress a gloating smirk as he strode forward, allowing his right knee to take his full weight; it felt as dependable and right as it had in years.

He was about to run upstairs when Kevyn's laughter floated to him on the crisp night air. Light and music and voices poured through the open corner window. He moved closer and peered inside. Miss Lucy was seated on a settee, her feet raised on a cushion.

"—and on the Movietone newsreels, they had been telling about men wearing ladies' clothing over their trousers so that folks would pick them up and give them a ride, and then those rascals would *rob* them." Miss Lucy tsk-tsked, her fingers moving steadily on the knitting or crocheting or whatever it was in her lap. He was relieved to see that she seemed fit and spunky, and he was also a little perplexed. She certainly didn't look like someone who had been so close to death's door that Kevyn had been unable to talk to him for a week.

"But Lillian was bound and determined to hitchhike, despite everything. She said she wasn't going to walk another step, and the next automobile that drove past, she was going to raise her skirt and show them that she didn't have on any pants underneath, so they would pick us up!" Kevyn's voice joined Miss Lucy's in peals of laughter.

Rusty edged farther toward the corner of the house until finally he could see Kevyn, lazing on the floor, her long bare legs stretched across the worn carpet runner in front of the fireplace. Still chuckling, she sketched madly, tossing her head in an attempt to get a long, curling strand of hair out of her eyes. His fingers itched with the desire to sweep it away for her, to tunnel into that glorious mane. . . .

"Did she? Stop a car, I mean?" Kevyn asked.

"Oh, no! Madeleine caught her arms and locked them to her sides—my sister Madeleine was always such a strong girl, you know—and while Lillian was trying to fight Madeleine"—Miss Lucy's voice broke into bubbling giggles—"I . . . I raised my skirt—just above the knees, mind you—and stopped a truck, just like Claudette Colbert in *It Happened One Night*."

"You didn't!"

"I did! It was a milk truck, and we got back to Baton Rouge and got the Packard repaired and in the carriage house before Daddy even knew it was gone!" She tugged at the afghan in her lap, and Kevyn leaped to her feet.

"It's getting too cold. Let me close the window."

Rusty stepped quickly around the corner. Damned

if he was going to get caught eavesdropping. Then he realized that his car was parked in clear view of the window. After Kevyn saw his car, it would look suspicious if he waited too long to make his presence known. He hurried across the front porch and rapped three times with the heavy brass knocker.

When Kevyn opened the door, the expression on her face was stunned, apprehensive—no, she was smiling, he realized. "Rusty! You're back from Washington? Did . . . did your game go well?"

"Really well, as a matter of fact." He took her hand in his; it was cold, but to touch her, however chastely, caused a warm reaction to zing through his body. "I wanted to check on Miss Lucy."

"Kevyn," Miss Lucy's voice called out. "Is that Rusty? Oh, do ask him in! I want to thank him for my bouquet."

Kevyn pulled him inside. It had to be his imagination that made him think she hesitated first.

"Young man, I simply have to tell you," Miss Lucy began the instant he entered the room. "I watched your football game on the television this afternoon." Her voice warbled with enthusiasm. "You were absolutely splendid, weren't you?"

He felt himself beaming. "Why, Miss Lucy, thank you. I didn't know you liked football."

"Oh, I don't. That is, I didn't. But I never knew a wide deceiver before."

He swallowed his grin.

"It was so exciting! But they hit you so hard, don't they? You must hurt dreadfully."

"It's not that bad tonight. Tomorrow morning is another story, though." He asked Kevyn, who now hovered in the doorway, "Did you see the game?"

"No, I was—"

"Kevyn was upstairs working," Miss Lucy said. "She's finished her painting, thank goodness. I can't tell you how relieved I am. I kept telling her that she should go back upstairs and finish her own business, that I was fine, just fine, but she wouldn't hear a word of it."

"Miss Lucy, please," Kevyn said. "We've been over this before."

"You're a sweet, sweet girl, but I spent enough years as a registered nurse to know that I didn't need such close attention for such an extended period of time." Miss Lucy pointed toward the sketch pad on the floor. "Let me see my picture now. I can hardly wait."

As he was several feet closer, and damned curious to boot, Rusty managed to retrieve the pad before Kevyn, though she made a game effort at beating him to it. She crossed her arms in front of her and tapped one toe while he flipped it picture-side up and caught his breath. Three young women from a long-gone era, clutching hats to their heads and skirts to their legs, fought wind and laughter as they leaned against a rickety wooden-railed bridge. One girl—after a moment's study he recognized her as a young, vibrant Lucy—had inched her skirt above her knee, exposing a perfect, plump calf. The sketch radiated joy and life, and he found himself not wanting to release it, but Miss Lucy held her hand out expectantly.

"Oh, isn't it lovely?" she crooned as she drew it into her lap. "Look—that's Madeleine in the middle. She had the wildest red hair and freckles, but the boys all loved her because she was lively. And Lillian. Kevyn, you captured Lillian as sure as if she were standing here—the way she stretched her neck that way. She was so proud of that long neck. Silly goose." Miss Lucy prattled on, and Rusty listened, captivated by her gleeful remembrances and by the rough sketch.

When she paused for breath he asked, "How did Kevyn know what they looked like?"

"Oh, we've done this many times before, haven't we, dear?" Miss Lucy patted the drawing affectionately. "Get my collection, Kevyn dear, won't you?"

"I don't think Rusty really wants—"

"I'd love to see them," he interrupted.

As Miss Lucy carefully tore the page out of the

notebook, Kevyn produced a large leather valise from a cabinet. "They're just a few sketches I've done for fun."

"My memories," Miss Lucy said fondly. "Kevyn makes memories for me."

Making memories. Rusty looked up at Kevyn, and remembered hearing those words before.

Miss Lucy pulled a stack of sketches from the valise. "Of course, Kevyn has seen my photographs any number of times. One day when I was telling her some tale or another, she began drawing the people for me—my people. Look, here's Percy." She pointed to a dapper young blade leaning against the fender of a classic roadster, goggles dangling loosely from his fingers. "That's my brother, Theodore's grandfather. Do you know Theodore?"

"Rusty doesn't know Simon, Miss Lucy."

"I haven't had the pleasure," Rusty confirmed.

"And this . . . ah, this. I believe I'm embarrassed." She tittered nervously, but Rusty found the picture captivating. A young man knelt before a young Lucy, his straw boater tilted back on his head as he pressed his lips against her palm. Her mouth was opened slightly, with an expression that led Rusty to believe that palm hadn't seen soap for days after. "My first kiss."

"Your first love?" Rusty asked gently.

"Heavens, no! That rogue kissed every girl in the county, and if rumors can be believed, he didn't stop at kissing some." Her crinkled eyes shone with humor. "But I do believe that a first kiss can be highly satisfying when it's delivered by someone who knows what he's doing."

"I should think so," Rusty agreed.

"Miss Lucy, aren't you ready for your orange juice now?" Kevyn asked.

"I do believe tonight deserves something a little stronger, don't you agree, young man? To celebrate your game?"

"I'm touched and honored, but I'm also in training," he answered. "Orange juice would probably be best for me."

"Kevyn dear, would you . . ."

"Of course." Kevyn patted Miss Lucy's wrinkled old hands and adjusted the afghan more snuggly around her knees.

She had no sooner left the room than Miss Lucy was tugging at Rusty's sleeve. "Come closer," she whispered. "I need to talk to you."

He knelt beside her.

"You must forgive Kevyn for being so skittish. She's like a mixed-up moth when you're around, darting away from the flame instead of into it."

"Flame?" Rusty asked, amused.

"Of course. You're the flame."

"And you're saying she's afraid she'll get burned."

Miss Lucy drew him closer. "She's afraid she might find out she likes the heat."

Rusty found himself laughing out loud, and Miss Lucy joined in. Kevyn reentered the room carrying a tray with three glasses of orange juice. "What do you two have your heads together over?"

"We were just discussing the fact that somebody needs their thermostat adjusted," Rusty responded.

Miss Lucy slapped his shoulder and chortled.

"Do you need another afghan?" Kevyn placed the tray on a tea table beside Miss Lucy's settee.

"Oh, go on, dear. You'll drive me silly if you don't stop hovering over me." Miss Lucy presented a cut-glass tumbler to Rusty, then one to Kevyn, and took the last for herself. "How about a little toast?"

"To your continued good health?" Rusty asked.

"That's too mundane. How about, to the season?" Her face lit up. "Your football season. May it be"— she slid her glance to Kevyn and back to Rusty again—"enchanting."

Enchanting. The last word in the world for his sport, his career. Yet, gazing into Kevyn's face, he found himself repeating, "Enchanting."

"Enchanting," she echoed as the three glasses clicked.

He added one more toast. "To dancing near the flame."

Kevyn fumbled with the lock, and was relieved when the door finally swung open and she could enter her own home. But footsteps at the bottom of the stairs stopped her. "I—I thought you were gone."

As Rusty ascended the stairs, he emerged from shadow and into silvery moonlight. His face was a contrast in blacks and whites, angles and contours, and as always, she wanted to record this moment on paper or canvas; as always, she wanted to touch, to stroke, to press her lips against those eyes, those cheekbones, those lips. She fought to still the response. But all of her uneasiness about their relationship, her need to slow down, seemed to recede as he stopped two steps below her, his face almost level with hers.

"I sat in the car until you left Miss Lucy's," he said. "I've waited all weekend—all week—for this moment."

He stroked her hair from her face, cupped her head to pull her nearer, and kissed her, a soft blessing of a kiss, a whisper of sensation as their lips brushed.

"This is what I've waited for."

She stood there unable to speak, thinking, *This is what I'm afraid of?*

Rusty pushed Kevyn's door open with his knee and took her hand to bring her inside. "I brought you something from Washington."

"The Washington Monument?" she said lamely as she locked the door behind them.

"Wouldn't fit under my seat." He stood behind her, massaging the base of her neck. "You've had a rough week, haven't you?"

"Hmmm . . ."

"You've done a great job, though." He rolled her shoulders, rubbing and squeezing, until she felt as if she would melt into his hands from the sheer ecstasy of his touch. "Miss Lucy looks wonderful. If I hadn't known, I would never have believed she'd been so sick for so long."

Kevyn felt a twinge of guilt stiffen her shoulders. "She bounced back rather well, didn't she?" She moved away from him. "You—you brought me something?"

Grinning, he fumbled with the zipper of an inside pocket. "Here, catch."

He flipped a small bar of hotel soap at her, and somehow, she managed to catch it.

"Good reflexes, lady."

"How thoughtful." She tossed the soap aside, laughing. "You certainly went to a lot of trouble. All this for me?"

"Nobody else." His eyes softened, and she shrugged. "I got kind of tied up and didn't get a chance to shop. Are you insulted?"

Kevyn shook her head in confusion. "You didn't have to bring me anything."

"I wanted to. I just wish I'd had time to really find you something nice." He ran his fingers through her hair, mussing it into unruly waves. "But I have something else." He led her into the parlor and was about to pull her into his lap on the chaise lounge when Demon leaped ahead of them and arched his back, digging his claws into the worn brocade fabric.

"I'm sorry." Kevyn grabbed a match, but Rusty took it from her.

"Allow me."

Kevyn shooed Demon out of the room as Rusty lit a branch of tapers. "I'm beginning to acquire a taste for candlelight." When he turned to face her again, he seemed a little hesitant, yet eager. He drew a small folder from another jacket pocket. Placing it in her hands, he said softly, "This is for you."

"What is it?" Kevyn opened the folder and found an oblong piece of paper with diagonal pencil strokes and shadings centered on it. "Did you do this?" she asked cautiously.

"I did it for you."

"Very abstract." She took out the sheet and angled it to better catch the light. "It's interesting. It has a strange kind of symmetry, in its own way." She held it vertically. "But this works better. Are you sure it wasn't supposed to be . . ." She broke off as she met Rusty's gaze.

Carefully, he took the paper out of her hands, turned it to the proper position, and gave it back to her. "It goes like this, Kevyn." But there was a subtle change in his voice, an intensity, an attentiveness as he watched her, that made her suddenly uneasy.

"Of course," she said. "You're right." What was he looking at? Why was he looking at her that—*No*. She knew that look. She knew that look. She knew that look. . . .

"Kevyn."

Her heart pounding, she couldn't tear her gaze away from his.

"It's your brother's name. I made a rubbing at the Vietnam Memorial for you."

The paper in her hand was fluttering. She couldn't hold it still. Rhett. It was Rhett's name. *Think about that—not the expression in Rusty's eyes.*

"Kevyn?"

She mustn't crush the paper—the precious paper. The ache rose in her throat as she smoothed the page, touched the lighter markings . . . Rhett's name, there on a memorial for everyone to see. She choked back the tears; she mustn't get it wet. She slid it into the folder.

"Kevyn," Rusty said, "you can't read."

Eight

Kevyn clutched the folder to her chest. Rusty was staring at her, staring with shock, amazement . . . she knew that look, and the scorn and the pity and the derision that went with it. Why wouldn't her hands be still? She placed one foot in front of the other and blindly pushed past him. Get out. She had to get out. She didn't realize she was running until she slipped and skidded on the hardwood floor in the darkened studio. She caught herself on the wall, jerked a French door open. He was coming behind her, but she slammed the door and flew deeper into the shadows, hiding from even the moonlight—but he was behind her still, behind her, too fast, too quick, and she was hiccuping with sobs that wracked her body, with pain that ached in her chest.

Then he grabbed her, spun her, and she struck out at him and caught his cheek with a limp fist. "Let go! Leave me alone!"

"Don't do this!" He wouldn't release her. He held her despite her twisting and pulling. "Kevyn, listen to me!" She steeled herself for one last effort, and for a moment thought she was free, but as she tumbled to the floor, and he with her, all she could think of was protecting the folder—don't let it get crushed—don't let—

"*Kevyn!*" He was gasping beside her on the ground. He wasn't holding her down now. "What's wrong? It's not that big a deal! I didn't mean to upset you!"

She couldn't move, could only fight for air and stare into the branches of the trees, into the sky beyond. " 'Not that big a deal'! Do you want to know why my brother died?" Her voice sounded hollow, disjointed, even to her own ears. "He died because he couldn't read."

"I—I don't understand."

"Of course you don't," she said viciously. "How could you? Or any of the others, the ones who said he was *stupid*. 'No good dropout.' That's what they called him. And when his girlfriend's father kicked him out of the house and told him never to come back—that he was worthless and lazy—he left and joined the army." Tears stung her eyes, her throat, as the words came pouring out. "They were getting killed over there! I was so angry. I was only nine, but I *knew*. How could I not know? It was on the television every night! Little figures that showed how many men had died every day, every week— and films, and pictures, and—and—oh, God—it was awful. And I hated him. I hated my brother for leaving me.

"And he died. He was a grunt, and he couldn't be anything else because he couldn't pass the tests . . . and he died."

"Oh, baby." He reached to pull her into his arms, but she wouldn't let him.

"Don't hold me. I don't want you to hold me. I want to be alone."

"I want to take you there, Kevyn. I want you to see." His fingers rubbed gently in her hair, but he didn't touch her. "I just wanted you to know. I didn't mean to upset you."

Her whisper a hoarse rasp, she asked, "It was really there? His name was really there?"

"It's there, Kevyn. I touched it with my own hands."

"Then it *is* over, isn't it?" she asked quietly.

"Kevyn. Why couldn't he read? Why can't you read?"

Why didn't that question strike fear and anger in her? She had spent it all, she supposed, for now anyway. She turned her head away from him. "He was . . . I am dyslexic."

"You see things backward."

She squeezed her eyes shut with the old frustration. "No, Rusty, I don't see things backward. *Things*—trees and sky and, and you—I see just fine. But words, letters, and numbers on a page . . . they're a jumble of scratchings. I can usually tell if something's a word or a number. Some are longer than others. Some have pieces that stick up or hang down. And what I recognize one day, I probably won't the next."

"You can't read at all?" he asked tenderly, and she heard, and hated, his pity. "How did you manage school?"

"I didn't." She pulled upright, leaves clinging to her hair and sweater. There was no disguising the bitterness in her voice, in her heart. "Got that? I didn't. When I was fourteen, I just stopped going. When I was nineteen, Simon took me to a special school in Dallas, where they tested me, and lucky, lucky me. I'm one of the few—the ones whose dyslexia is so extreme, it can't be overcome."

"I—I can't believe that there isn't anything that can be done."

"Of course you can't. You think I don't know that? You think that I haven't seen it in people's eyes— 'She could do something about it if she put her mind to it.' "

"I'm sorry, Kevyn. I didn't mean it that way."

She heard his chagrin, his remorse, and knew how intensely he hurt for her. But that didn't help. There was nothing he could do to help. Atticus understood. Simon had understood. Miss Lucy understood. The only way they could help her was to help her maintain a life where she could believe she was normal.

"You know, Kevyn, there was a time when I thought I was pretty hot stuff. A big-money contract and all that attention—I started thinking I deserved it. One thing you have to remember in my business—you never deserve it. You're lucky if you can get it, but there's a difference between luck and worthiness." He shrugged. "And the flip side. No matter how bad it is—you don't deserve that, either. That was the hardest to accept. When the press came down on me—and I really had been a jerk—I started believing that too. Crazy, huh? I believed them when they told me I had the greatest hands in football, and I believed them when they said I was dog meat. It took me a long time to realize the truth. That I was neither. I'm just me. Rusty Rivers. Nothing more, nothing less. What remains to be seen is just how good Rusty Rivers is." He smiled, but his smile was touched with bitterness. "I wasted a lot of time believing other people. It's only been recently that I started believing myself."

"I suppose you're telling me—"

"I'm not telling you anything. What happened to you, and what happened to me, are as different as night and day. But . . . well, if it helps, it's there.

"Kevyn." This time he touched her, and as he touched her cheek with his fingertips, she felt more comforted than distressed. "You have the most beautiful eyes I've ever seen."

She turned to look at him and saw in the moonlight that his own eyes were moist.

"You do," he said. "There's no way to compensate for what they don't do for you. I know that. But when I see your art, I feel awed. And when I look into your eyes, I get lost in them."

"It's not my eyes," she whispered. "It's . . . the dyslexia's in my brain."

"There, you see? I knew it couldn't be your eyes. . . ." He traced her lashes, tickling them, making them flutter, then touched them with his lips. "*Vrai ravissant.*" His breath wisped warmly through her hair. "*Je t'aime, ma chéri.*"

"What did you say?" she asked. "What does that mean?"

"You're very beautiful, and I love you."

Before those words—those momentous, precious words—could soak in, he was pulling her to her feet. "Let's go inside."

She was too tired to protest, and yes, too overwhelmed with something that felt frighteningly, amazingly like love.

"Mornin', darlin' . . ."

Slowly emerging from a heavy haze of sleep, Kevyn rolled over and faced Rusty's drowsy smile.

The room was still cloaked in a netherworld of shadows. Yet a ray of sunshine managed to find its way between the magnolia leaves and through the window, spattering over his body, casting him in a warm Rembrandt glow.

She nestled back into the pillow. "Good morning."

"You wouldn't have anything as mundane as a clock in here, would you?"

She closed her eyes and stretched. "It feels like it's . . . ummm . . . about nine."

"Is this always the way you tell time?"

"I'm not usually up this early," she admitted. "Clocks have no meaning in my life."

"Oh, I didn't . . . didn't think about that." He seemed genuinely chagrined. "You can't read a clock?"

"Of course I can. I just don't pay any attention to them."

He groaned as he rolled over and tried to sit up. "Too bad Coach Bigelow can." His face contorted with pain as he clutched his side and attempted to swing his legs over the edge of the bed. "This mattress is too soft." His bare feet touched the floor, and he stood up, only to fall back on the bed with a grunt.

"Can I help you?" Kevyn asked hesitantly.

"Yeah, you can stay out of my way. Once I get

moving, I'll have to depend on forward momentum to get me to the john."

"Oh." Eyes wide, she leaned back against the dark mahogany headboard and watched him struggle to an almost upright position. Then he hobbled around the bed and out into the hall, his hands pressed to the purplish bruise on his ribs. It wasn't until the bathroom door closed behind him that she let out her breath. How could he live this way, barely able to walk in the morning?

Who was she to judge the way a person chose to live?

She sat on the edge of the bed. *Chose.* Maybe that was the difference. He chose to live this way, when he had a dozen other options. He had a college education, a background rich in opportunity, intelligence, and health. She had never known anyone who had all the advantages, the potential, everything it took to lead a storybook life. Rusty had.

He still did. And maybe that bothered her as well.

She had never fit in with people like Rusty. Her parents were a generation older than the parents of her schoolmates; thus she had always found herself drawn to the maturity, the wisdom, the understanding of age. Rhett's friends had doted on her, tossing her in the air and allowing her to tag along occasionally when they hot-rodded their way into the countryside to fly through the cotton fields and occasionally scale an oil derrick out of the sheer exuberance and foolhardiness of youth. It was only among little girls her own age that she felt cast out and ridiculed, and as she grew older, among young men her own age that she felt so strange as to be singled out as "weird Kevyn" and "that geek."

She didn't know how to deal with people who thought she was abnormal, who acted as though she were underprivileged.

She shrugged on her robe and began brushing her hair. She had never meant to tell him about her . . . problem. Her—Lord, she hated the word—disability. She wasn't ashamed, only protective.

It wasn't anybody's business.

And she was uncertain how she felt about Rusty's discovery. She wasn't comfortable with it, not at all. She felt as if some vital part of her shield, the protection that she had built for herself, was missing, and that she was totally dependent on the benevolence of someone new, someone unproven, to help her maintain what was beginning to feel like a fragile balance between coping and not. It made no difference that of course he would never tease or ridicule, and it made little difference that he seemed to accept her situation without *too* much pity.

She tossed the brush onto his pillow with unnecessary force. She had simply never intended to get involved with this man, had never intended to care. . . . And that was the problem. She cared, and she wished she didn't. She skimmed her hand over the warmth on his side of the bed, and it felt good, so good. Disturbingly so.

By the time Rusty emerged from the bathroom, Kevyn had made a quick trip downstairs to check on Miss Lucy and take care of her own ablutions, as well as borrow some peach preserves. She had pulled on a pair of work jeans and an old shirt, and was making the bed.

"Nobody should look that damn good in the morning."

She eyed his obvious agony and felt helpless to understand. "Nobody should look that damn bad in the morning."

"Well," he growled, "it's an honest living." His dark eyes grew thoughtful. "More or less." Then his face brightened. "I wish you'd have seen the game."

"No . . . I'm sorry." She tried to keep her voice level. "It's difficult for me to follow."

"Maybe I could help you . . . if you want?"

He had slipped his hand inside the open collar of his shirt and was rubbing his shoulder. When his hand dropped away, she saw an ugly bruise, and had to fight hard to keep from reacting to it, as he obviously paid it little attention at all. "I don't think so," she said. "I'm . . . really dense about things like that. It would just drive you crazy trying to teach me."

"Why don't you let me be the judge of what will drive me crazy?" Rusty dropped to the side of the bed, straining to pick his trousers up off the floor. "I took some hits yesterday. I guess you can tell." He struggled into the soft brown cords and then rested, pale.

"It must have been awful."

"It was fantastic." He grinned, *look ma, no hands!* in his eyes. "You should have seen me. I took everything they dished out and more. Eight receptions for one hundred and seventy-two yards. Not a bad day's work. And, if you'll forgive me for boasting, I am now in the Gents' record books." He flexed his large hands. His voice dropped and sounded . . . almost wistful. "I made the first touchdown ever scored by the professional football team otherwise known as the Louisiana Gentlemen."

Kevyn crossed to his side and stroked the shadows under his eyes. "That's wonderful," she said doubtfully.

Something tense and impenetrable hovered between them, almost tangible in its force. Then a wry smile twisted one corner of his mouth. "Well, it's nice of you to say so, anyway." He shrugged on his shirt but left it unbuttoned. "Where's the paper? This is one morning when I don't have to be afraid to open the sports page."

Kevyn tucked a strand of hair behind her ears. "I don't take the paper. But Miss Lucy does. I'll call down and get hers." She pulled away from him and went into the kitchen. She was dialing when Rusty came up behind her.

"No papers, no clocks. There are advantages to the life you lead, lady."

"It's a nice place to visit," she said shortly. When Miss Lucy answered, she asked, "Could I—we—borrow your newspaper, please?" Rusty's arms snaked around her waist. "Just send it up in the dumbwaiter," she said breathily as he tickled the nape of her neck. "Thanks. You're a sweetheart." She hung up the telephone and rotated out of his arms in one movement. "I know you're running late, but do you have time for breakfast?"

"Hell, I'm late so often that the coach would think I was sick if I showed up on time. And I'm starved." He nuzzled her ear. "Like, bacon-and-eggs kind of starved." He tweaked her bottom. "And thighs-and-legs kind of starved." She whirled toward him in agitation, only to find him leaning against the wall and smiling dreamily. "Damn, I was good. I wish you could have seen me."

She placed the flat of her hands against his chest and pushed him toward the door before he could melt her defenses. "You get your paper. I'll fix breakfast."

She was peeling strips of raw bacon off the package and laying them in the old iron skillet when Rusty reentered the kitchen, the *Journal* in one hand, a small stack of envelopes in the other.

"Your mail," he said.

She stared at the large brown envelope on the bottom of the stack and finally recognized the emblem on the return address. She dropped the last two pieces of bacon in the skillet and rubbed her hands on the seat of her jeans. "I've been waiting for that," she said. "Just put it down. I'll take care of it later."

"How do you read your mail?" Rusty asked.

"Atticus comes over every week or so and reads it to me. If something looks important, I take it down to Miss Lucy."

"Artists. It's a good thing you don't live in the real world."

Kevyn's hand froze at her throat. She forced herself to meet his gaze. "This is the real world—my world."

"Sure, I didn't mean to offend you." He looked troubled. "Isn't . . . isn't there any way I can help you?"

For how long? she wanted to ask. *And then,*

when you're gone, what do I do? But these were questions she dared not ask. They came with answers she didn't want to hear. She carefully thumbed through the envelopes until she found the South Central Bell Telephone bill. She pulled it free and slapped it in Rusty's hand. "You're worried about my mail? Here. Make yourself useful. Break the bad news to me while I rescue the bacon—unless you like it blackened?"

"Hardly," he said, ripping into the envelope. "Not too bad. Thirty-eight twenty-five." He gingerly lowered himself to a cane-backed chair and rested his elbows on his thighs, the bill dangling from one hand. "You should have seen my bills when I lived in Buffalo. Heat, telephone—they ate me alive."

Kevyn flipped the bacon and grabbed eggs from the refrigerator as he launched into ice-cube memories of upstate New York in the wintertime, the mail a dead issue.

Over breakfast, Rusty peered across the table, a quizzical expression on his features. "And you really expect me to believe you were an ugly duckling?" He bit into one of his six pieces of bacon and chewed thoughtfully. "Impossible."

"I have the pictures to prove it." Nursing a cup of black coffee, Kevyn watched him dig into the mountain of food on his plate. "I was always skinny. Then when my hair started changing—" She shrugged. "Kids are cruel. But you get over it."

"Yeah. I know." He pushed a piece of muffin through the peach preserves on his plate. "So, when did the transformation take place?"

"You can't figure it out?"

"I guess not."

"I was a late bloomer—very late. When I finally 'bloomed,' it came as something as a shock." Her voice changed subtly as she weighed her words, measuring them cautiously lest they have the wrong effect. "It was Simon who did it for me. You've seen the portrait."

Rusty's fork hovered over the plate, and his muscles tautened. "Oh, really?"

"The butterfly coming out of the cocoon. Corny, huh?"

He stared at her intensely, his food obviously forgotten. "I don't guess I quite thought of it that way." He put down his fork, took a deep breath, and said, his voice teasing, his eyes deadly serious, "I don't have a chance with you, do I? I can't paint you a picture, I can't write you a sonnet—I'm not part of this world you chose."

His words were too close to the truth, but for all the wrong reasons. For that reason—and no other, of course, no other—she sprang to reassure him. "Don't be ridiculous." She sipped from her coffee, meeting his gaze steadily. "Simon was an artist. That's what artists do. I was Simon's momentary inspiration. If it hadn't been me, it would have been someone else."

Rusty pushed to his feet, wincing a little as he straightened. But more than anything else, he seemed relieved. He dropped a kiss on the top of her head. "Now, I have to deal with something even more unpleasant—an angry coach. I'm late, as usual."

Kevyn slid out of his embrace and stood, offering her hand. But as she handed him his jacket, his pockets gaped open and their contents clattered to the floor.

"Don't move—I'll get it." She dropped to the floor and found a pill bottle under the edge of his chair. "What's this?"

"Dope," he answered casually.

Slowly, she picked it up. She felt the blood in her veins turn to ice. She tossed it at him, noting that despite his condition, his reflexes were excellent. He caught them with an economy of movement that came from finely honed instincts, and years and years of practice.

"Hey, I didn't mean to upset you." He glanced at

the label and pointed to the prescription. "Codeine. The legal kind."

As if she could read it.

"They hope that if I take enough of it before next weekend, I'll forget how bad I hurt this morning and be ready to do it all over again."

"Do you want some juice to help you swallow them?" she asked, trying to keep the strain out of her voice.

"Kevyn, lighten up. I don't take the stuff. See?" He indicated the date on the label. "I've had this since summer training camp, and it's still full. This is the first time I've worn this jacket since then, I guess."

What was wrong with her, that she felt washed with relief to know he avoided drugs, when he so obviously was in pain? "What do you do when you hurt?" she finally asked, retrieving his car keys and some loose change.

"I used to kick my dog. Now, I just lie in the whirlpool and cuss a lot."

It took a moment for the twinkle in his eyes to register, and Kevyn felt her face soften into a smile. "You'd better hurry."

"Yeah, I better." He ran his fingers roughly through his tousled auburn hair.

She reached for his hand and their fingers twined, and she asked the one question that had hovered in her mind for weeks. "Have you ever forgiven me for kidnapping you from the triathlon?"

"Nope." But his eyes sparkled with humor. "Never interfere with a man and his desire to prove himself. The male ego is a fragile thing." His voice softening, he added, "I'm glad I was ready for you when you found me. A year ago—"

"You wouldn't have been interested?"

He snorted his derision. "Not interested? A year ago, I would have ditched the race and kidnapped *you*. Like I said, I wasn't ready." He tossed his jacket and shirt over his shoulder and made for the door, his limp noticeably less pronounced.

"Rusty—"

He waited for her to continue, his eyes questioning.

"They—they won't be hitting you today, will they?" She couldn't disguise the tremor in her voice. Desperately, she dropped her gaze to her clenched fingers.

"Not today," he responded gently. "I'm okay. *Really.*"

She watched his slow progress down the stairs, watched him fold painfully into his car, and then watched him grin and wave and drive away.

Kevyn cleared the table. As she left the kitchen her toe sent something shiny skidding across the floor. Nudged between the chair leg and the wall, a ring sparkled in the sunlight.

A chunky gold and diamond ring. A man's ring. She picked it up carefully, awed by the weight of it, the size of the stones. She realized two things: It was Rusty's Super Bowl Ring; it was etched with dried blood.

Gingerly, she held it between her thumb and forefinger. Somehow it seemed to embody everything that threatened, that confused her about the man. Uneasily, she placed it on the table.

No. It seemed too valuable to simply leave out in the open. She glanced at the glass-paned kitchen cabinets, at the row of coffee mugs; she dropped it inside the one on the end, closed the cabinet door, and stared at it.

No. It made her nervous leaving it there.

She palmed the ring, its weight an ominous thing . . . then she slowly slid it on her finger. She remembered the girls in high school who had worn their boyfriends' tape-wrapped senior rings. She felt silly, unsettled, trying on a feeling that she hadn't considered in so many years: belonging. She had longed to belong, not just to a person, a steady beau, but to fit in and have all the social ramifications that went along with wearing a boy's ring, dating, being accepted.

She supposed, aware of a niggling little if-they-could-see-me-now imp sitting on her shoulder, that Rusty's Super Bowl ring certainly had more clout than all the rings of all the boys who never looked at her except to snicker put together. She supposed there was a time when such a thing would have meant the world to her. She knew, without supposing, that those days were long gone.

She slipped off the ring and finally, unwillingly, stuck it in her jeans pocket. Its weight on her thigh offered her no comfort. In fact, it seemed to galvanize her to move forward, to do the things she needed to do.

She walked into the studio and pulled the large Kurzweil envelope from the bottom of the stack of mail. She eased out the brochure and studied the pictures, and once again experienced the thrill of anticipation. She was so close. . . . She wouldn't have to depend on anyone or ask anyone's help. With the scanner and the voice simulator, the machine could actually read for her, and who would have to know?

She snatched the drape off "Darius," which was completed and awaited only her signature to be ready for shipping. In a few weeks she should receive her check from Fantasy Books.

Even after the bills she had to pay, with the money from this painting her bank account would finally register ten thousand dollars. It had been a long, frustrating task, saving that money, but now that she had it a new independence difficult for her to imagine was within her grasp.

She crossed the room to the small cubbyhole formed between a stack of clean canvases and the peeling wall. She pulled a sketch pad out of its hiding place and sat cross-legged, brushing her hair out of her face. Languidly, she turned pages one by one until she found those first sketches of Rusty. They had a vibrancy that surpassed any image she'd ever captured with mere pencil and paper before.

Why should she still feel this way, when every line,

every shading was committed to memory from hours of study? She could no longer delude herself. It wasn't the sketches, the artistry, or the technique that held her spellbound.

It was the man.

Her fingers had traversed the contours of that face—the high, slashing cheekbones, the heavy brows, the curling lashes. Her lips had tasted the saltiness of his flesh and the drugging power of his kisses. Nowhere on the paper before her was anything that warranted the reaction she'd felt from the beginning. Yet, just seeing these brief, rudimentary sketches was enough to open her up to his power, to make her relive the desire she'd experienced in his arms.

She had an urge to pick up a pencil, to record the memories she had imprinted on her mind for all of eternity. But, for the first time, she was intimidated by a project. She felt totally inadequate for the task of capturing his untamed spirit with the tools of her art. It was like trying to record one dazzling stroke of lightning as it split the cloak of midnight. A camera could capture its form, an artist could capture its intensity, but no media could capture its dizzying power.

Her eyes lifted slowly to the wall of artwork, resting on her own portrait. Is this what Simon had felt when he'd painted her—the need to seize that perfect moment of their relationship and preserve it for the time when it would be over? If so, he had failed. His work was beautiful and technically splendid, but it lacked life. His painting lacked the emotion that it should have had, if it had been a testimony to their love. Unless . . . unless what had been between them had never been love. It certainly wasn't the full-blown passion she'd experienced in Rusty's arms. There had been compassion and tenderness, but perhaps there had never been love.

That thought would have shocked her a few weeks before. She'd always believed in the utter transience of "love," that feeble emotion that swelled into bud like a blossom, burst into fragrant flower, and with-ered and died, to be swept away with the hot, dry winds of summer.

But now, she experienced feelings that didn't blos-som—they raged. Instead of being sweetly filled, she was hungrily yearning for more.

She touched the tip of her finger to the flat white page in her lap, brushing lightly over the pencil marks as if expecting to feel the sparking sensation of life flow into her again. But there was only the cool, smooth, lifeless paper.

And in her pocket, the heavy, cold weight of gold.

Nine

"Well, Dad, what's the verdict?" Rusty watched his father's face cautiously for any subtle variation in the noncommittal doctor's mask he wore, and saw none.

"I agree with the team doctor." His father made a few notations on the chart. "I wouldn't put any weight on it for the next forty-eight hours, keep up with your physical therapy, and by this weekend you should be ready to play."

Rusty didn't realize how relieved he was until the tension eased from his body in a huge sigh. "I can't believe the Redskins gave me their best shot, and I walked away laughing—and then my own cleats do me in, in practice, no less. I planted my foot to pivot, and the tread of my cleats decided it didn't want to let go of the turf—and the next thing I knew, I was on the ground staring at sky."

"That's the problem with artificial turf. I'd be glad to see it go the way of the Edsel, myself. Get back to real grass and mud. It's hell on the grounds keepers, but a lot easier on joints and athletes." The phone on his desk buzzed. "Excuse me a minute, son."

Rusty idly scanned his father's office while the older man took the call. Immaculately decorated in masculine shades of gray and wine, the room was dominated by a single framed poster behind his father's desk: Alexandra Petrova. The black and white photo was over thirty years old, yet his mother's artistry, her vivacious, almost abandoned pose as "The Dragonfly," the playful angle of her head and coquettish smile on her finely sculpted features were unmistakable—he was never able to view the poster without smiling.

"And she gave it all up for you, you big lug," his dad said, completing his call.

"I thought she gave it up for you," Rusty countered.

"She gave it up because she was thirty-three and her days as a prima ballerina were numbered, but it appeals to her sense of the dramatic to believe she gave it all up for love, so we'll continue to humor her, eh?" His dad chuckled, smoothing his graying auburn hair from his temples. "That was the hospital. I need to check on a patient."

"Dad, just one more thing." Rusty toyed with his knee brace. "What do you know about dyslexia?"

"Dyslexia?" His father began removing his lab coat. "What does dyslexia have to do with anything?"

Rusty felt the telltale flush creeping up his cheeks. "There's a girl, a woman I've been seeing. She has dyslexia, and I just wanted to find out more about it."

"A special girl?"

"Oh, Dad." Rusty groaned.

"Okay," the older man relented. "Dyslexia is pretty far removed from my specialty, but basically it's a neurological disorder centered in the brain. It's an inability to recognize words, or spell, or to understand what's read."

"Kevyn can't read at all. She was told that hers is a rare case that can't be helped." Rusty dug his fingers into the upholstered arm of his chair. "I don't know, Dad. I feel so helpless. There has to be something that can be done."

Dr. Rivers shrugged into a sports coat and slipped a fedora on his head. "Sometimes . . . well, sometimes help comes in different ways. Just because you can't 'fix' something and make it all better, doesn't mean you can't help."

"I guess I'm learning that." Rusty eased out of the

chair and reached for his crutches. "And yeah," he added, grinning, "she's real special. Just don't say anything to Mom yet. I'm not up to her third-degree interrogations at the moment."

"Just a minute." His father picked up the telephone and punched in a number. "Helen? Call down to Dr. Ferber's office and see if they can gather up some information on dyslexia. Tell them Rusty will be stopping by to pick it up in a few minutes. Thanks."

"Who's Dr. Ferber?"

"A psychologist on the third floor. She ought to have some literature that will—"

"Dad, a psychologist? Kevyn's not—well, she's not—"

"Disturbed? Of course she isn't. But the first order in diagnosing a learning disability would probably be a psycho-educational analysis of some sort." He held the door so Rusty could maneuver through. "You're getting pretty good on those crutches. Let's don't make a habit of this, okay?"

Rusty grunted. "I agree two hundred percent."

Was she really spending more time sitting alone in darkened rooms with only the candle flames for company, or did it just seem that way? Since Rusty had left that morning, Kevyn had felt restless, uneasy. As dusk fell, she felt drawn to carry her hot lemon water into the parlor—not the bedroom, for the memories in the bedroom offered no comfort—and to light the candles, though doing so sent Demon skulking to his cushion on top of the refrigerator. Lately he had seemed a little resentful, and she supposed that yes, she had been spending more evenings surrounded by quiet and dark and flame. Guiltily, she snuffed the candles, went into the kitchen, and sidled up to the refrigerator. Demon blinked at her, then averted his head, his twitching tail the only sign of life.

"Well," she said crisply, "do you want company or not?"

One eye opened to a slit, and he stretched a paw out in front of him, then another, as if each limb had to be wakened separately. Finally, when she was about to call off her efforts at companionship, he stood on all fours, arched his back, and climbed gingerly onto her shoulders.

"I wasn't going to beg you, you know," she grumbled, stroking his head as she started back to the bedroom. But the telephone rang and Demon leaped from her shoulders, leaving sharp jabs of pain where he'd used her flesh for leverage. She grabbed the receiver.

Why she clutched the lump in her pocket simultaneously, she couldn't say. But somehow Rusty's voice didn't surprise her.

"You must have been sitting on top of the phone."

"I was close by." She held the ring in her fist. "I was wondering when you'd call."

"I know, I know." He sounded weary, beleaguered. "I should have called you sooner, especially after you gave me that terrific breakfast and . . . and everything. But things got a little out of hand, and I'm only now recovering."

"Out of hand? What kind of things?"

"Just a little twisted knee. No big deal."

She shifted her weight uncertainly. "Which knee?"

"My right."

The ring cut into her palm where she was squeezing it. "I thought you'd be looking for your ring."

"Is it missing?"

"I have it here. It must have fallen out of your pocket."

"Thanks. I hadn't noticed." Silence dragged out between them. "I . . . I jammed my finger in the game in D.C. and it wouldn't fit over my knuckle."

"Anytime you want to come get it is fine with me."

"I can't drive very well. But if you could come over here to my place—" His voice took on more vitality. "That's it. You can come over here. And you can bring the ring, and we'll talk, and . . . gosh, that sounds great. Best news I've had all day."

"You'll have to give me directions," she said. "I don't know where you live."

"Sure. You won't have any trouble. You just come into Lakeshore Drive and—"

"Lakeshore? Rusty, where do you live?"

"I live on Willow Point."

"You mean, you live *on* Lakeshore Drive?" She twirled a strand of hair around her finger.

"I've been meaning to talk to you about this." His chuckle radiated into her ear, and she felt a shiver of delight, despite her best intentions. "The triathlon was practically in my backyard, you might say. My house backs up to the lake."

"So that day, when I brought you home with me, I could have taken you to your own house."

"In a fraction of the time."

"But you weren't in any condition to tell me that," she said primly.

"Be honest, Kevyn. If I had said—which I tried to do—"

"You didn't say anything. You were practically unconscious."

"But not totally. And even if I had said, 'that's my house,' would you have stopped?

"Of course not."

"So you kidnapped—"

"Rescued!"

"—me. Never mind. I give up."

Kevyn frowned as she turned her little VW onto Willow Point, a mossy, pine-covered peninsula that jutted into Cross Lake. Lately a heavier foot on the gas pedal, not to mention crossed fingers and held breath, were necessary to get the little car to accelerate. A tune-up and a new muffler would have to wait. She absolutely refused to dip into her savings now. Not when she was so close to her goal. The moment the check from Fantasy Books came, she was prepared to place the order for her Personal Reader.

She carefully counted the houses until she found Rusty's. A rustic contemporary wrapped in rough-hewn cedar and stained a rich sienna, it was an older home on a small lot backed up to the lake. Kevyn got out of her car and walked across the yard.

On the porch, Kevyn started to rap on the huge oak door, only to have it swing open, seemingly of its own volition. Immediately, Rusty appeared, his hair slightly ruffled, his expression almost bookish behind a pair of tortoiseshell framed glasses that seemed a calculated Clark Kent disguise. Only nothing could disguise the broad shoulders under the bonze plaid shirt, the strong thighs under the baggy trousers.

Kevyn saw the crutch. He leaned against it, his injured knee slightly bent and wrapped in some sort of protective foam shell. The strain around his mouth seemed to loosen, as if her mere presence filled him with satisfaction. "Damn. You look good."

"I was going to say something similar. Expletives deleted."

He nudged his glasses up on his nose. "Sorry, it's been that kind of day."

"I didn't know you wore glasses."

"Just for reading. I've been studying my play-book." He frowned. "I wish I didn't have to. It's a real pain in the—" He shot her a sheepish look. "A real pain."

"Oh." She had difficulty dragging her gaze away from his crutch. She thrust her hands into her slacks pockets. "Aren't you going to ask me in?"

"Oh, sure. I'm sorry." He hobbled out of her way. "You found me okay?"

"You give good directions."

"I run great pass patterns too." He laughed at her confused expression. "Forget it." He closed the door as she stepped into the small foyer. A skylight high above spilled a muted haze of light into the alcove, illuminating a lacquered Chinese screen, black with a golden dragon stretching across its three panels.

"This is beautiful," she said.

"Yeah, it is, isn't it? I blew a bundle on it my rookie year on a road trip to San Francisco. I shipped it back to my mom, and she almost died. By the time I got this place, I'd sent her so many odds and ends that she was threatening to hold an auction just to clear her house out. Come on in and sit down. I've got something to show you." He led the way, managing the step down into the dimly lit den with only minimal difficulty. As he stumped lightly over the wide expanse of tile floor to the conversation grouping arranged around a massive rock fireplace, she realized: *This man is no stranger to crutches.*

He settled into the corner of the sectional and propped his injured leg on an ottoman, then patted the spot beside him. "You look wonderful. Just what I need to make a hell of a day end up right."

Kevyn glanced around as she sat beside him, suddenly and strangely ill at ease. The entertainment center on the wall was filled with expensive-looking stereo equipment and a large screen TV. The furniture was buttery-soft leather, the rug under their feet plush Oriental. How much money did a wide receiver make? Obviously enough to continue the storybook lifestyle his parents had started for him.

"You have a beautiful home."

"Thanks. I'm just getting used to it, to tell you the truth. I lease it from a friend of my dad's. I never bought a place of my own. My career hasn't exactly been a bastion of stability."

He flipped on the light beside him. Then he lifted a stack of papers from the end table. "I've been doing some reading." He cleared his throat. "About dyslexia. How long has it been since you were tested?"

"Eight years." Kevyn felt tension coil in her stomach. "But believe me, you don't outgrow it."

"I know that, but listen, teaching methods are changing. I read about this guy, he was a businessman—a successful businessman. And no one knew he couldn't read, because he had surrounded himself with secretaries and gofers to handle all his paperwork. But one day he decided he wasn't satisfied anymore, and—"

Kevyn closed her eyes. *Wasn't satisfied anymore.*

"—he went to adult reading classes and the teaching volunteer kept using different methods, until one day she tried a new one." He twisted toward her, winced, and grabbed his knee. "Ouch! I'm getting carried away." He massaged his leg and continued, "Anyway, this new method—this—" He motioned with the paper in his hand. "This visual phonics is kind of like sign language. It gives you something tangible to associate with the symbol on the page, so that you can remember, say, an *A* as much by the way it feels when you do it, as by the way it looks. This guy I read about literally signs each letter or word as he's reading aloud, and it's very slow, but he's really reading, and getting better at it."

"Rusty, please. I—I appreciate the fact that you went to so much trouble, but I—I—"

"Baby, this isn't trouble." He stroked her face and pulled her closer. "I want to do this. I want to help you. In fact, I'm sure I can find a good doctor or school or something, and if a volunteer teacher can help this man, then I'm volunteering to help you." He touched her lips. "We could at least try."

"As if I haven't already." Her words were so softly spoken that at first she thought perhaps he hadn't heard.

Finally he laid the papers aside. "I didn't mean it to sound as if you've never tried."

"I know."

"Kevyn, you've got nothing to be ashamed of."

She felt the breach between them widening, and could only laugh to keep from crying. "You don't understand. I've *never* been ashamed of being dyslexic. I was ashamed that I was stupid, that I couldn't read, that I was a failure. I was so ashamed that I sometimes . . . sometimes I wished I'd never been born.

"Lord, Kevyn."

"But when they told me I was dyslexic and explained what that meant—for the first time, I *wasn't* ashamed. I was relieved, because I wasn't stupid, and didn't have to feel that way. And angry—angry that nobody had figured it out sooner. Angry that my teachers didn't figure it out. But they hadn't been trained to recognize the symptoms, so how could they? And angry at my parents for not pushing harder, for not taking me to doctors or whatever it took to find the truth. But they didn't know any better, either. It wasn't their fault. It wasn't *any-body's* fault."

She tilted her face up to his, imploring him to understand. "Rusty, I'm normal. Not being able to read is *normal* for me. It hasn't stopped me from doing anything that I wanted or needed to do. It's only when people make me feel *not* normal that all of the pain comes back and all of the old wounds open up. So I simply don't allow myself to get in a position for that to happen." Then, her voice quavering with emotion, she repeated, "I am not ashamed."

"Kevyn, I've never known anyone as strong as you."

"Sometimes surviving looks like hiding." She twisted her fingers in her lap. "Sometimes it even feels that way. When you have to depend on someone else to read you a letter or write a check out for you or keep your bank accounts straight." She swallowed hard. "But I really didn't come over here to talk about any of this. You . . . you said you had something to show me?"

"Yeah." He seemed as relieved as she felt to change the subject. "Mind if I show off a bit?" He pressed a remote control beside him and the television and VCR clicked on. Then he tugged lightly at her shoulder and pulled her back against him as the tape began.

"This is the Washington game. That's me, eighty-

six, middle of the screen." The camera zoomed in
for a close-up, and she recognized his movements
as he ran down a football field of churned-up mud.
The camera angle changed, and he was leaving the
ground, sailing into the air, twisting, twisting. The
ball suddenly appeared in his upstretched hands. He
pulled it into his chest, landed, and hit the ground
running. By the time any other players came near,
he'd slammed the ball into the ground and was surrounded by other players in gold and gray, leaping
and slapping one another on the helmets.

He paused the action on the image of a single fist
pumped into the air from the center of the mob—
his fist.

"This history-making moment is brought to you
by . . ." He laughed, but she could sense his pride,
his exultation. "'After five games, we finally scored a
touchdown. *I* scored a touchdown."

"One for the record books," she said thoughtfully.
"Show me again."

"Sure." He rewound it and started it again, and
this time as she watched, a cog fell into place. "That
jump. It's like your dancing, isn't it?"

"Of course. I can do a hell of a slam dunk too."
He pointed to his shins. "See that? Like built-in
springs. My elevation has always been my strength.
All the years I danced, the purest happiness I ever
knew was when I leaped." He smiled. "It's the closest
thing to flying I can imagine—the control, the movement in midair. Flying."

"And you do a lot of it in football."

"Running and jumping, my stock in trade." He
stopped the tape and fast-forwarded. "Our next possession, I made another pretty decent catch. Let me
see if I can find it." He stopped and started, searching through a confusing jumble of football images.
"Good, this is it," he said. Again, the camera caught
him walking from the huddle, bending over, then
suddenly springing forward and running down-
field—funny how he limped a little when he walked,
yet he ran like a gazelle—only this time when he

flew into the air to grab the ball, another player seemed to emerge from nowhere and leaped after him. They tumbled to the ground together, and a third player hit the pile—and plowed his helmet straight into Rusty's ribs.

Kevyn flinched and went cold as she thought of the bruises, the blue-and-purple bruise she had seen. She kept her eyes trained on the television through sheer willpower and a desperate desire not to let him see how distraught she was. But the screen seemed a blur; she couldn't have said what happened next. Luckily Rusty was intent on giving her a play-by-play analysis.

"That, dear girl, is what is known as spearing. Illegal. It usually brings a fiteen-yard penalty for unsportsmanlike conduct. If the ref calls it. He didn't."

She swallowed a lump in her throat. "I see."

"But the most important part of that play? Watch." By this time she could focus enough to see two bodies on the field. The player in the red-and-gold uniform stood up, grabbed Rusty's hand, and pulled him to his feet.

"Polite bastard," Rusty muttered, then froze the picture again. "See that? I still had the ball. That's the important thing, whatever else happens—they can break your knees, knock your head off, turn you upside down . . . but as long as you hold on to the ball, you've beat 'em, and they can't stand it."

Her mouth dry and palms damp, Kevyn forced herself to avert her attention from the television. *Oh, Rusty,* she thought pensively, *what goes on in that head of yours?* She tried to reconcile the athlete, the savage, with the boyish male who tugged at her heartstrings, or with the man who collected antiques, however erratically or impulsively, and had once, ever so long ago, been a dancer in the element of illusions and dreams.

Which one are you? she wanted to ask. *Which one is real? Please tell me, so I'll know who I'm dealing with, who I'm loving.*

She could dismiss the memories of the wounded warrior returning from a tragic and glorious defeat, limping and bruised and aching. Lying in the circle of his arm, it would be simple to do.

"Rusty," she said desperately, cutting him off in mid-description of yet another bone-crushing hit. "Could we . . ." She stared at his full lower lip, at the crease down its center, at his woodsy-green eyes and glorious red-and-gold hair and remembered what a work of art he was in the sunlight—all warm colors and magnificence. She must remember that, think of that, concentrate on that, not the physical abuse that disturbed her and frightened her.

"Rusty," she said again, and he took her hands in his. Her hands were cold, so cold, but he was so warm. . . . "Rusty, could we . . . could we . . ." She couldn't say it, so she did it. She leaned into his body, raised her lips to his, recognized the flare of response in his eyes the instant before they kissed. Slowly, his tongue probed the recesses of her mouth. So slowly his hand slid down her back, skimmed around her rib cage, and eased up to tease the underside of her breast. So, so slowly, his other hand reached for the remote control, hit a button, another button, and finally turned the television off.

"I didn't want you to think this was the only reason I invited you here," he murmured into her hair.

But she refused to think about those other reasons. She reached for the top button on her blouse and opened it. She moved to the next, and, his eyes darkening, he stroked a strong, callused finger between her breasts.

"You do know how to make a man forget his aches and pains," he said as she opened yet another button.

She ground her teeth in frustration, biting back her response. How could she make him understand—she needed to make herself forget his aches and pains. After the last of the buttons came free, she took his hand in hers and showed him.

She inhaled deeply and felt herself swelling against the constraints of her lacy black bra, and watched his face as she moved his hand to the nipple, already hardening at the thought of his touch. And when he touched her, even through the lace, she felt a charge of heat sear into her. She caught her breath, licked her lips, and when she saw him watching her . . . licked them again.

She raised to her knees and reached behind herself to unfasten the clasp, and somehow, not even remotely accidentally, her breasts were within inches of his eyes, his lips . . . and before the bra could fall free, he seized a throbbing peak with his lips and began stroking her with his tongue, a tickle of warmth and wet against lace and flesh, and then the rasp of his teeth, and she got her wish, for suddenly there was nothing in her world except the exquisite sensations this man sent sizzling through her. Her breath came in quiet gasps as she gave herself over to his torment . . . and then a loud intake of air when he pulled away and blew . . . blew across the nipple that strained against its barrier and ached for more. He peeled the bra from her skin, and his lashes fluttered and his lean cheeks tautened as he dipped his head and took her into his mouth again.

"Ohhh . . ." Words wouldn't form. She was going to . . . going to die if he didn't stop and . . . and . . . She pulled away from him, the sound and feel of suction breaking coursing through her and when he raised his heavy-lidded eyes to hers, she desperately guided his lips to her other breast and gave herself over to the sweet agony.

His hands, strong hands, cupped her bottom, raised her, shifted her, until she was straddling his lap, and then he feathered his fingers down her back, making her arch into him as he took more of her into his mouth, and she moved despite herself, a slow writhing that grew in intensity as he closed his teeth, ever so lightly, over the tip of her nipple, licked her, tormented her . . . and she was lost, lost in a haze of desire, captive of her need. Low moans, little whimpers, they were hers, and she could no more stop them than she could stop breathing. And then, she felt the heat of her desire responding to pressure, hard pressure, and felt the bulge she was writhing against. She jerked and would have pulled away, but his hands, his strong, strong hands, circled her hips and held her there. And then the pressure, the rubbing, the writhing chased everything from her mind except the blind pursuit of completion.

Desperately she fumbled with the fastening of her jeans and somehow managed to get them off. She reached for him and realized he was still fully clothed and she was naked, and as he pressed moist kisses against her stomach, she didn't even care. "Please." She took his face between her hands and stopped him. "Please." She moaned again, and groped for and found the evidence of his arousal.

His hands were no more sure than hers when he loosened his belt, unzipped his jeans, and shifted to release himself. She stroked him, felt him throb in her hand, and her knees went weak. She kissed him with tiny, frantic kisses, and tugged at his shoulders to pull him over her, but he stopped her.

"Not like that," he ground out. "Not with my knee."

His knee. She squeezed her eyes shut and clamped her lips on a broken sob. Even in this, she couldn't forget, and when he spread her legs and thrust into her, she wasn't ready, wasn't ready, and a gasp tore from her throat. Anger and rage warred within her, anger at him for not being what she wanted him to be, and rage at herself for being such a fool. . . . She was sobbing weakly, and gulping, holding her body stiff, but his movements beneath her were dissolving her attempts to hold on to the rage, turning them into something else . . . something hot and breathless and pulsing.

Tears filled the depressions around her eyes and ran down her temples to dampen her hair. His fingers brushed the moisture out of her eyes. "Oh, baby . . ." She felt his lips dragging across her cheeks, the coarseness of his skin against hers, the gentleness of his touch. "Don't be afraid of loving me," he begged. "I won't hurt you. You've got to believe that."

Then his mouth joined with hers, suckling at the fullness of her lower lip, his tongue then dipping into her mouth, plumbing her depths in an erotic mimicry of the physical union that joined them. Gone were thoughts of pain and fear. All she felt was a myriad of sensations spiriting through her, sensations springing not just from his actions, but from the caring and tenderness he transmitted with each touch.

The buttons of his shirt abraded the sensitive skin of her breasts. He kissed them softly, rubbing his face and his thick tangled hair across them until the nerves became so tender, they hovered on the threshold of pain. Then, hearing the moan that gurgled low in her throat, he returned to their crests to lathe his tongue across the throbbing peaks, a warm and moist comfort that sent waves of pleasure melting through her body, and she tightened around him and moved on him.

Even as he uttered love words against her neck, his fingertips feathered down her body, dancing circles on her inner thighs, and instinctively, she quickened her action and he groaned in response. He raised his body to meet hers, and they moved in a synchronized rhythm as old as the act of love itself, each movement a delight of satin abrasion, driving her upward and upward toward that dizzying pinnacle of release. When she thought she could bear no more, the tightly wound coils of throbbing sensation began spiraling through her, and he drove into her, until she was plummeting into a black abyss where all she felt was him inside her, filling her, and at last, at last . . . easing her gently back down to the firm ground of earth.

"Would you like to tell me what that was all about?' he asked afterward, his voice hoarse and gravelly.

She turned her tearstained face up to his, her eyes

deep and shadowed, and he felt her withdrawing from him. "I—I can't explain. I'm so confused." She buried her face in his chest and shook her head, the movement swirling her silken abundance of hair against his chin. "You don't understand."

He tightened his arms around her and fought the tension that was tightening around his gut. He had to be patient, not push, but patience had never been his strength and pushing had always been his way, and for once he was determined to get to the bottom of whatever was bothering her. So he spoke, his words sounding harsher than he'd intended, "You're damned right I don't understand. So why don't you try explaining to me?"

She jerked away from him. "Please don't be this way."

"What way? Don't be what way?" He grabbed her blouse and thrust it at her. "I want to know what's going on, Kevyn. I want to know what it is that makes you cry when you're in my arms, what kinds of ghosts I'm chasing."

"No ghosts," she whispered. "Not like that."

"Then make me understand. What is it you want from me?" His hands drew into fists as he tried to control his anger. "Why did you come here?"

She trembled before him, groped for her clothes, and plunged a hand into a pocket. "I came to give this back to you." She dropped the ring in his hand. "I came because . . . because you sounded like you needed somebody."

She was looking everywhere but at his face, and he grabbed her chin and forced her eyes to meet his. "Not somebody. You."

"Don't be angry. I don't want you to be angry with me." Her eyes brimmed with tears. "I didn't want it to be like this."

"Kevyn, don't you understand? You *made* it like this." He dragged his fingers through his hair, kneaded his thighs. "And the damnedest thing is, I don't even care. I just want to know why."

"Rusty, what happened between us . . . I don't understand it. It's so beautiful and terrifying."

"Why? Why terrifying?"

"Because I don't want to hurt again," she murmured.

"This all makes sense to you, doesn't it?" he asked wearily. "You try to close me off so that I won't hurt you. Tell me, does self-inflicted pain hurt any less?" He was startled when she had an answer for what he had thought was strictly a rhetorical question.

"Yes. It does. Because I can control it." Her voice trembled as she began pulling on her clothes.

"Tell me, dammit. Tell me what it is that I'm up against!"

"You'll never understand—you and your always-had-it-all life! Maybe you're one of the lucky ones, maybe you *will* always land on your feet. But that's all the more reason you'll never understand. You've never lost anybody. You've had everything, everybody—you just don't know."

"Oh, give me a break."

"Once, I was cherished. I don't know any other word for it—more than love, more than caring . . . I was always different. They used to laugh at me and call me names."

Rusty stared at her, incredulous at the thought, but she was beyond seeing him, still caught up in the past. "But the one place I never felt that way was at home. I was so sheltered, so protected. At school I was a nonentity, a weirdo, stupid. But at home I had my art, my dreams . . . like a cocoon.

"I was a change-of-life baby, an afterthought, and always realized that my parents were older than anyone else's. Sometimes I was so afraid that they would die and leave me. . . ." She raised her eyes to his, and they seemed to be asking questions that had no answer. "But it was Rhett. I—wasn't ready for it to be Rhett." She lifted a slender hand to her brow and rubbed, as if trying to erase the memories. "I wasn't totally unprepared when my parents died. Neither were in good health those last years. But suddenly, I was alone." Her eyes were shadowed, their depths haunted. She had only been seventeen or eighteen, he thought, and alone, unable to read or even function in the world. The idea of what she'd suffered tore at him with vicious stabs of pity. One loss after another—how many could a young girl survive without cracking? Was it any wonder she'd surrounded herself with fantasy, hiding from the real world and all its commitments?

And he remembered what she had told him. *I never loved anyone without losing them.* He wrapped his arms around her, stroking her, loving her. "I can't change anything that's happened to you. I can't promise nothing will ever hurt you again. Kevyn, I can't even promise that I won't hurt you." His hands tensed on her shoulders, and he forced her to look at him. "I understand why you're afraid. But you're missing a very important part of the equation. You're not the only one who can get hurt. You've already hurt me. Before this is over, you may rip my heart out, and don't think for one minute that you couldn't do it. But I have to have the answer to one question.

"How far are you willing to run?"

She tossed her head desperately. "I don't understand."

"You're running from me. You say you're running from pain, but I say you're running from *me*. And Kevyn, I intend to be behind you, every step of the way. Either we both win, or we both lose. But I don't believe in draws."

For the longest time she didn't speak. A log in the fireplace popped; the central heat clicked on, but no other sound broke the silence.

Finally, she shivered, and he pulled her close. She touched his cheek, her lips quivering. "You must believe in miracles."

"I have to." He didn't know what to do but simply hold her; somehow, holding her seemed enough . . . for now.

Ten

Kevyn stood before the canvas with tears of frustration streaming down her cheeks.

"No!" she cried, slashing out with a palette knife, ripping a diagonal slash from top to bottom. She crumpled to the floor, clasped her knees, and rocked. Nothing worked. Not a damn thing.

What had begun so many weeks ago as a yearning had become a compulsion. An obsession.

She had to paint Rusty. She had to capture him, slather him onto the canvas in strokes of color. Every image she had of him, from stark black-and-white-shadowed abstracts to moonlit and rain-dampened passion to soaring athletic leaps, had failed to materialize on canvas. She had searched her art books, had tried techniques and styles she'd never before attempted, with disastrous results. And each failed effort only honed the need to paint him to a finer edge.

But as she sat there, her cheek pressed against her knees and her tears spent, she thought of another image. . . .

She stood slowly, shoved the torn canvas aside, and replaced it with a freshly primed one. She picked up a broken piece of charcoal and sketched in a sweeping stroke, a shorter one, several more . . . then stood back and studied it.

He was kneeling, tense, waiting, his helmet beside him. . . . She scrutinized it. What was it about this pose—*this* pose—that seemed *right* when the others

weren't? The merest outline was there—not of
Rusty's body as she knew it by sight, by touch, by
taste, but uniformed in the battle gear she had
grown to despise, with impossibly wide padded
shoulders. . . .

Wide shoulders—armored shoulders. A stroke
down the center of his chest, and he wore a breast-
plate. Shoulderpads subtly transformed to shoulder
pieces and plates, thigh pads to cuisses, and the
face guard on the helmet at his knee, with a few
quick strokes of the charcoal, became a visor.

It wasn't dramatic. It wasn't terribly different from
anything she'd done before. And maybe that's why
it began to flow from her fingers, her imagination,
like quicksilver. A forest glade took form, rough
shapes that were exquisitely detailed trees in her
imagination. Her hand moved faster, she used the
heel to smudge a soft squiggle where mossy rocks,
mushrooms, shade-loving primroses would be. A
single shaft of sunshine would find its way through
the thick foliage to rest lovingly on the armored
shoulders of a kneeling knight. Arthur of the Round
Table—noble, pure, yet with an expression in his
eyes that seemed to foretell his future and the events
that would torment him.

Her charcoal poised, she stopped, staring at the
canvas, seeing it as already completed. A ray of gold
touched his locks with gleaming fire, defined his
highly sculpted cheekbones and illuminated his eyes
with the woodsy green of the forest.

She had found it. She was ready to work. Standing silently, she felt the fluttering in her breast that
said, *Yes . . . this is it.* She laughed, the sound exul-
tant in the large studio.

Sergei Rivers, I have found you. She plunged
headlong into her work, her desire, her obsession.
The need to put paint to canvas was a hunger
denied too long.

The sun was setting when she finally stopped and
studied her remarkable progress. "Not bad for a

beginning." She stretched, easing muscles that were tense and aching from hours of unbroken labor.

She turned the canvas to the wall, thrust her brushes in turpentine, and shoved her palette of oils in the freezer, too tired to do a more complete cleaning job. After coiling her hair atop her head and securing it with a large barrette, she peeled her clothing from her body and stumbled, exhausted yet sated, toward the bathroom.

Outside the windows, the early November air was chilled with the first snap of cold, turning the leaves to crackling colors ranging from fiery to earthen. But inside, hot water filled the claw-footed tub; lotus-scented steam billowed up in a vaporous cloud. Kevyn slipped into the water, her breath escaping in a soft sigh, giving herself over to the drugging sensation of heat on her tired body.

Her mind filled with sights, with sounds, with memories. These past weeks had been filled not only with frustration, but also with the presence of the source of that frustration. Most nights she and Rusty spent together. When he was on the road, he kept in touch, constantly surprising her. Once he'd called from a phone booth at the Metropolitan Museum of Art in New York City. He'd described the Rembrandts, Picassos, Monets . . . he had rambled on, filling her with his reactions, asking her questions. She'd laughed; she'd listened; she'd understood.

He'd brought her a miniature Liberty Bell from Philadelphia, a stack of jazz albums from St. Louis, and a Model T pencil sharpener from the Ford Museum in Detroit. Yet nothing matched that first gift, the rubbing of Rhett's name now framed on her bedroom wall. There was no substitute for a gift from the heart.

But memories that haunted also crept into her thoughts. Though his knees remained miraculously uninjured, the St. Louis game had left him with two disjointed fingers, swollen and purple for days. The Giants, too, had left their marks, as had the Eagles.

But hadn't Arthur had his share of battle scars? Surely he hadn't emerged from battle unscathed. When she squinted just so, she could see him kneeling, waiting, so valiant, so beautiful. . . .

She frowned and stirred uneasily in the water. Was this what she had come to, where her foolishness had taken her? Had she searched and searched, only to find a storybook image, she who had almost been Guinevere?

Rusty walked across Kevyn's yard, scuffling through the crackling leaves. His knee felt good—damn good, all things considered. He climbed the stairs more easily than ever.

He had news, hopeful news for Kevyn. This Thanksgiving game was in Dallas, which had started him thinking. He had hopes that this Thanksgiving would be very special indeed.

He knocked on the door, but Kevyn didn't answer. He pounded harder, then shrugged and started around the house to the studio. He had grown accustomed to her moods, her spells, the times when she was so deep in thought that she didn't hear and didn't see.

The French doors were unlocked. Stepping into the house, he found its warmth was welcome after the frigid outside temperature. The smell of turpentine still hung heavily in the air, but she wasn't working, so he walked into the hallway. The silence confused him, yet something kept him from calling out. Loosening the tartan muffler from around his neck, he walked slowly through the house, searching for her.

The bathroom door was ajar, and the humid scent of bath salts lured him inside. Kevyn lay in the tub, her eyes closed, with the peaks of her breasts and the caps of her knees poking out of the water. *His*, he thought with a wonderful sense of possession.

She stirred, sending the water rippling around

her, and her eyes fluttered open. "I didn't hear you come in."

"I heard you snoring halfway across the yard," he lied, unzipping his leather jacket. He dropped it to the floor, then sank down beside the tub. Crouching on his heels, he whispered in her ear, "You look good enough to . . ."

"Eat?" She smiled sultrily, her eyes deepening in color.

Marry, he thought in surprise. That was the word that had almost tumbled out. The word sent the blood singing through his head, leaving him dizzy at the thought. He gazed into the shimmering quality of her teal-hued irises, their power threatening to pull him in deeper than he'd ever been before. Her breath fanned across his cheeks, and their gazes met, a caress no less potent than if it had been physical. Finally, his lips brushed against hers, lingering at the corners of her mouth before pulling away.

Watching her, he sat with his back against the wall.

"I'm almost through," Kevyn assured him, lathering her sponge.

"That's okay. Take your time." *Marriage,* he thought desperately. *Permanence. Roots.* He wanted it. He wanted her. And in wanting, he found himself in a position he had never anticipated. He picked up one of her scattered sketch pads, a pencil, and to mask his emotion, his thoughts, he pretended to doodle, moved the pencil point across the roughly textured page in circles, spirals, arcs. . . .

As their weeks together had passed, he'd grown so dependent on her. They never discussed football anymore. It was a forbidden subject that he feared broaching, feared because he could see her doubts in her eyes. But that was the glory of it. The pencil stilled in his hand. Sure, he sometimes felt ready to burst with pride at the way the team was changing, the way he and Skipper were turning into an enchanted duo—Skipper throwing the bombs, and

Rusty catching them. Sure, he wanted to share those feelings. But it didn't matter. For there were even more times when he came to her empty, dejected, hurting. Again, football wasn't discussed. Being with her was enough. They shared a life away from football, away from the world. And it was a life he could picture sharing for a long time, even forever.

He lifted his head to look at her. She was still skittish. Sometimes there was a clouded expression in her eyes, a mood he couldn't dispel. He could only try to understand, try to provide her with the same unselfish solace she gave so abundantly to him. That was why he couldn't speak to her of permanence . . . of marriage . . . and especially not of the school in Dallas. Not now. Not when he felt as if it would only take one wrong move, one misunderstood word, to send her skittering away behind the walls of her "normal" world.

Loving her was like trying to catch a moonbeam in his hand. As long as he held his hand still, it rested, silver and shimmering in his palm. Yet he didn't dare close his fingers, for fear he would catch not the light, but only the dark emptiness where it once had been.

A mess of scribbles covered the page in his hand. And in the middle, he had drawn a stick figure as a joke. After all, she had drawn *him* in the tub. But it wasn't funny. Somehow, it made him feel sad. Lines and circles, and kinky curlicues of hair, totally void of life. He didn't have her magic touch. He didn't know how to breathe life into a lifeless form.

A spatter of water sprayed the page as she rose and grabbed her towel. His hands closed over it first, his fingers sinking into the deep black velour. Then he slowly, lingeringly, rubbed it over her moist skin. "Yeah, now that you mention it, you do look good enough to eat." He lifted her out of the tub and carried her toward the bedroom of the midnight sky and the winged horse.

She said he believed in miracles.

He didn't—yet he desperately needed to create one.

"Rusty . . ." His name was half-groan, half-plea on her lips as he suckled her nipple.

"Hmmmm?"

The vibrations zinged right through her, stealing her breath and setting off tingling fires between her thighs.

"You wanted something?" he asked.

"What's wrong with you tonight?" she asked on a sigh, even as she parted her legs to allow his fingers passage. "You—you're so tense."

He stopped his caress for a moment, and she saw a shadow cross his face. Then the rhythmic, sliding, probing movements of his hand began again. "You need to ask?"

She arched her back, clutched the sheets, bit her lower lip—that hadn't been what she meant, but she no longer could form coherent thoughts as he drove her higher with lips and fingers, until her release was a hoarse cry and a long series of shuddering, quaking convulsions. Her bare skin still quivered with tender aftershocks when he murmured in her ear, "Kevyn . . ." and teased in a raspy voice, "I'm still tense."

She knew not what caused the shadows, but she knew how to drive them away. She slid down his body, found his urgent need, and stroked and teased until his muscles were hard knots of iron, his hands clinging to the headboard behind him. And then he filled her with his passion and his seed. And again, her response pulsed around him as his strokes slowed, slowed, slowed, until she thought she would die if he didn't stop, and would surely die if he did.

And when she could finally think and breathe again, she bent close to him, took a strand of her hair and laid it across his upper lip, and said, "You would look funny with a mustache." She flopped over on her back and asked him yet again, "What's wrong?'

"Nothing you want to hear about."

"Oh." She splayed her hands before her eyes and watched dust motes float between her fingers. "Must be football."

He didn't answer at first. "Yeah . . . you're right." But he had hesitated just long enough to make her wonder.

"What is it, then? Tell me. I *want* to hear about it. I promise."

He seemed doubtful, and when he finally answered, she still had the uneasy feeling he was avoiding something. "San Francisco."

"Oh, Miss Lucy said they're good."

He chuckled mirthlessly. "You might say that."

"And you're worried that they'll beat you."

"You little nitwit, I *know* they'll beat us. I'm used to that."

"But you don't like it."

"I don't like it," he said. "Now we've talked about it. Let's find something better to talk about."

She reached slowly for an old, tattered book from beside the bed. It was several moments before she could bring herself to ask. "Rusty, would you read to me? There's a story in here I want to hear."

He seemed startled at first, took the thick volume from her hands, then started laughing. *"Le Morte D'Arthur?"*

"I just want to hear your voice," she said, yawning and nestling into the crook of his shoulder with a secret smile. "Read to me about King Arthur."

"First," he said, and she raised back up, "can you . . . can you read any of the letters?"

Her first impulse was just to say no and be done with it. But, because he seemed so earnest, because his voice seemed curious but not judgmental, she finally placed her index finger on the book cover and pointed. "M . . .O—O's are easy. Is this . . . is this an L?"

"T," he corrected gently.

"I get them mixed up." She lay back against his chest. "Aren't you going to read?"

"*Le Morte D'Arthur*, by Thomas Malory." He opened the book to the first yellowed page.

She sighed contentedly. "I wish it were in French."

"You don't speak French."

"Like I said, I love to hear your voice. . . ."

What a day. Never had a portrait come together so quickly. Every detail, every nuance flowed from Kevyn's fingertips.

No knight in shining armor, this man. His armor wasn't shining, but tarnished and encrusted with grime. He was no Galahad, no Lancelot, but Arthur, a man of the earth, a man who had put honor before everything.

As before, she had lost all perspective. Just as the early sketches had tantalized and tormented, the portrait itself held her spellbound. Was it good? She didn't know. She didn't care. When she looked at it, it lived, it breathed. In all honesty, she admitted, Arthur was the excuse. Rusty was the reason.

She heard his car and turned the canvas to the wall. Rusty had been at a Boy Scouts award banquet and was coming in late. The moment he entered, he scooped her into his arms and spun in a circle with a joyous whoop. "I feel great!"

"Rusty!" she gasped. "Your knee!"

He eased her to the floor. "You worry more about my damned knee than I do." He bounced like a boxer, itching for a fight. "See? I've been doing my mom's exercises. Wouldn't the press love to get hold of that info?"

"I can think of someone who'd kill for a scoop like that," she countered wickedly.

"I'll just bet you do." He pulled her to him, tilted her face to his, and kissed her. "I've got a surprise for you."

"Surprise? Where?" She felt inexplicably uneasy,

and suddenly his exuberance seemed a mask over some tension she couldn't quite place.

"How would you like to spend Thanksgiving weekend in Dallas? A friend of my dad's has a suite at Texas Stadium, and he invited my parents for the game. But they can't make it, so I thought if you wanted to go . . . after the game we'll have until Sunday night to do whatever we want."

"Why, that's—that's—" Kevyn groped for words that sounded grateful, and if possible, excited. "I'd love to get away for a few days," she finally said. "A very romantic weekend, just you and me."

"Yeah, real romantic." He searched her eyes for a moment, then seemed to force a smile. "I need to study awhile. Do you mind?"

"Of course not." They went into the parlor, where Rusty reclined on the chaise and Kevyn sat at his feet with a sketch pad. As usual, the lighted tapers, strategically placed, kept Demon sullenly at bay.

Kevyn gazed up at Rusty, immersed in his playbook, a frown knitting his brows. Glasses perched on the bridge of his nose, he'd almost pass for a scholarly professor, were she to ignore his wide shoulders and leanly muscled physique. But why would she ever want to ignore them?

Slowly, she peeled her sweater over her head. With a sidelong glance in his direction, she reached for the clasp that would release her breasts from their lacy confinement, and remained poised, awaiting his comment.

"You know," he remarked, never looking up from his book. "The Cowboys' secondary is one of the most dangerous in the NFL . . ."

"Mm-hmm," she murmured, still waiting.

"When I line up at the line of scrimmage for a post play, even after the play's called, I have as many as five different options, depending on what I see in their defense. If the linebacker goes one way, I cut inside; otherwise, I run straight ten yards and pivot, unless of course their corner's on me, in which case I have to feint in, then out—" He raised his eyes to hers, and from their blaze she realized he had known all along. The playbook slid from his hands. "In which case I tackle you to the floor and ravish you."

"That's some playbook," she remarked, as her black lace bra fell away.

"Yeah, especially when it leaves me room to improvise," he countered huskily.

He had to tell her. Kevyn lay in his arms, trailing her fingers over his chest, so utterly at peace that he found it, as usual, so much easier to avoid the issue altogether.

But this time he couldn't. Someone had to force the issue, and he supposed, considering the appointment he'd made that afternoon, that someone was him.

"Kevyn, I've got to talk to you about Dallas."

"Could we go to the top of that tower? The one with the restaurant on top?"

"Reunion Tower? Sure. We can even stay right there at the Hyatt Regency if you want to."

"Emerald City." She sighed.

"Wh; ?"

"The Hyatt Regency has always made me think of Emerald City."

Merde. This was going to be more difficult than he'd anticipated. "You plan the weekend. We'll do whatever you want and . . ." Why had he said that? With the plans he'd already made, did he really think letting her choose the hotel and restaurants would assuage her?

"Why don't we skip Dallas?" She continued to stroke his chest. "Skip your game. Skip the whole world. You know, just you and me, and let the rest of the world go to Hades in a hand basket. Now that would be something to give thanks for."

He closed his hand over hers. "I've made some plans for Friday." And, to get it over with, to finally get it out in the open—"I've arranged for you to be seen at the Cromwell School."

Her body turned to ice beside him. Slowly, she withdrew her hand, her arms, her very soul. "You did what?" Each word came out clearly, distinctly, as sharp as if sliced from a thin sheet of glass.

"Kevyn, I called them yesterday. It just seemed to me that it's been so long since you were evaluated, that something may have changed—not in your condition, but in the prognosis."

"Oh." She sat up and pulled the sheet around her body. "So that's the way it seemed to you."

"Oh, jeez. I'm botching this for sure," he muttered, grasping the corner of the quilt to maintain some covering for himself. "I just wanted to know if I was right. I wouldn't have even brought it up if I'd been wrong, but the therapist said that there was every possibility that with new learning techniques—"

Kevyn sprung to her feet and walked away from him.

"Look, maybe I should have asked you first, but when she offered to see you Friday, I thought it was too good an offer to turn down. And—and—" His frustration welled up in him. "Dammit, Kevyn, if I'd asked you, you would have just said no. So I told her I'd have you there, and I intend for us to go."

She stood at the window, her back to him.

He snatched his briefs from the foot of the bed and tugged them over his hips. "All I'm saying is that the therapist said that one's late twenties is the prime time for people like you to begin to be able to get the help they need. Sure, you had a rough time when you were a kid in school. That's typical. But now you've had some time to put it in perspective. Maybe, just maybe, this time it'll work. This time we'll make it work. Together."

"Tell me, Mr. Rivers, after you cure me of my *affliction*, what plans do you have for Saturday? Do you heal the sick and walk on water too?"

"Oh, give me a break."

She whirled to face him. "That's exactly your problem, Rusty. You've had *all* the breaks. You have no concept of what my world is like—you with your talent, and your big-money contracts, and your education, and—"

"I didn't finish."

"What?"

"I didn't graduate from college. I spent my four-year tour of duty there, and then I went to the pros. But I never got my degree."

"Am I supposed to feel sorry for you?" She was incredulous. "Rusty, it seems to me that every single opportunity you've had, you've tossed away because you couldn't be bothered. *You couldn't be bothered!* Well, I haven't had your breaks, your opportunities, and I hope you'll forgive me if I find it hard to sympathize."

"You think you're telling me something I haven't figured out on my own? You think that every day I'm with you I haven't become more aware of what I've squandered, while you've taken on an obstacle that's so large, I can't even imagine it? You've somehow managed to accomplish more for yourself than I've ever dreamed of. Kevyn, you're my inspiration! I've realized that I have to take this chance, this one chance, to make something of myself, and it starts right here with the Gents. I've got to prove to myself that maybe I really was as talented as they claimed I was. Because you know something? Deep down I've always been afraid that I wasn't. And—and—I thought, if I could just help you *somehow* overpower your problem that I could repay you for what you're doing for me. That I could give you something nobody else has been able to give you. I thought if you would at least give it a try . . ."

"If I would just give it a try . . . As if I haven't tried, and tried, and tried. As if I spent my life waiting for some damn knight in shining armor to show me the way to solve all my problems."

"Maybe . . . maybe I spent my life . . . waiting for somebody who needed me to be that knight. For somebody who needed me to be strong for them, because I haven't done a very good job of being strong for myself."

"Rusty, what do you want me to say?"

"Say you'll go and at least give it a try."

"At least give it a try." She was silhouetted in the moonlight and shadows, and as she turned her profile to him, he had the most absurd vision of her struggling to emerge from a cocoon again. "At least give it a try," she repeated softly. "I could do it if I just tried, is that what you're saying?"

"That's not what I mean, and you know it, Kevyn."

"All those years of trying and being laughed at—and trying and failing and finally quitting because if I tried one more time and failed, I wouldn't survive." He couldn't see her face in the shadows; Lord, he needed to see her face, but he was afraid to move, to speak. "I don't know if you understand what I'm telling you, Rusty. *I wouldn't have survived another day of it.* This fourteen-year-old girl stood in front of a mirror with a razor blade, and found herself looking at it as if it held an answer, a way to end the misery."

"Oh, Lord . . ."

"Don't 'oh, Lord' me! I threw it away! I simply threw it away and said nobody, *nobody,* is ever going to make me feel this way again! I'm not stupid, and I'm not going back to that school, I'm not facing those people, *I'm not giving them the power to make me feel this way again.* Do you understand what I'm saying?"

"Kevyn, I love you so much, that even the thought of what you're saying . . . Kevyn, I'm sorry. I'm sorry. I was wrong." He felt tears clogging his throat, and didn't care, because he had to know, had to know, "Have I—do I make you feel that way?"

"No. You never make me feel that way." And then she crumpled into his arms. "Just hold me, Rusty. Just hold me."

He took great gulping breaths of her perfume and tightened his arms around her. "Please forgive me.

I never wanted you to be anything else. You've got to believe that. I wasn't trying to make *you* be different. I wanted to believe that together, we could be even more than we are apart." And as he held her in his arms, this most precious thing he'd ever known in his life, he realized what had been hidden to him before. The strength of her love for him had changed him, not by force, but by allowing him to be what he was. These last games, when he had accomplished what he'd always dreamed of, had happened because he had finally accepted the challenge within himself after years of running from it.

"Kevyn," he whispered, "be who you are. Just be who you are. But . . ." he couldn't stop himself from adding, "be sure you *know* who you are. Don't turn your back on the possibilities."

The whole of Texas Stadium rocked with the Dallas Cowboy anthem; the home team had just scored. And the private suite where Kevyn sat was no less jubilant. Jeans-clad men and women with diamond-encrusted fingers, and those dressed in designer fashions, all joined in the raucous celebration. The score: Cowboys 10, Gents 3.

"This here's gonna be one helluva ball game!" Gander Bodine boomed, bending over Kevyn's seat. "And it's too damn bad that Rusty's mom and dad have to miss it. I know your boys are gonna put up one helluva fight. And boy oh boy, do I like a good, rough ball game!" He tilted his glass to his lips and took a healthy swig of Scotch. "Hope you don't mind if we yell a little louder for *our* boys than we do for y'all's." He grinned, exposing a mouthful of gold inlays.

Kevyn could only smile stiffly and turn her attention back to the field. How different it was from her first game, where she'd sat huddled in the cold. Now she reposed in the lap of luxury. Tilting forward in the deep blue-upholstered swivel rocker, she watched

Rusty pace the sideline, his tension evident even from her lofty perch. His helmet under his arm, he cocked his head toward the action.

Finally, he got his call. With an immediate straightening of posture, he jerked the helmet on and ran onto the field, fastening his chin strap as he jogged along. Joining the huddle, he bent over. Breathlessly, she riveted her eyes on him. She couldn't watch. She couldn't turn away.

Heat. Cold. Rusty experienced both and cared about neither. The crowd noise was a dull roar in his ears, yet he heard Skipper shouting the sequence . . . or was it instinct? No matter. He knew. Staring across the line of scrimmage, he considered the men in silver and blue, then dismissed them. The snap, the pitchout, and he was running, cutting left, then right, feeling the twinge in his knee but ignoring it. This was it.

He could taste six points. They were his.

Be there, buddy, Skipper had said. *You get open and look up—I'll do the rest.*

The twenty-yard line—the fifteen—the ten—and no one around. *I'm open!* Rusty pivoted. The closest Cowboy was still fifteen yards away. He had him beat—he had him beat—but where was the ball? Frantic, he looked up and found it. *Too high! Dammit, Skipper—too high!*

He saw the assurance in the other player's stride. *Tough luck, sucker,* it seemed to say. That was all it took—that assurance. Rusty sprang up, flying higher, reaching—and he felt it—the sting of pigskin and laces hitting his palms—the heat—the surge of adrenaline. Desperately, he pulled the ball in and tucked it into his body. He was falling, landing—

And the pain was excruciating as his knee gave way. *Not now—not now!* Pulling to his feet he felt the pain, but the Cowboy defender was closing in on him. Five yards to go—then two—then the end zone, and the hit. Every joint in his body screamed in protest as two defenders landed on him. It didn't matter. They were too late. He had scored.

Gratefully, he sank into the cold, echoing blackness of oblivion.

Kevyn jumped to her feet in shock. Why wasn't he getting up? Pressing the damp palms of her hands to the cold glass window, she felt isolated, stranded with her fear. She watched as players began to crowd around, blocking Rusty from her view. Then the doctor and the coaches arrived. *What's happening?*

Gander moved to her side. Kevyn spoke in desperation. "He'll get up—he always does." Then, staring back down at the field, "He never quits."

"Sure he will, honey. That boy of yours is a tough one. He probably just got the wind knocked out of him." The man's voice lacked conviction, and watching the confusion on the field, Kevyn felt the chill of fear wrap over and around her.

"Talk about a foul-up," a loud voice exclaimed from the television on the wall, "the Cowboy secondary got stung!"

"Don't be too hard on 'em, Pat," the second commentator remarked. "Watch this replay. First you'll see Rivers looking for the ball . . . here it is—watch this!"

Unwillingly, Kevyn faced the small screen. She felt a sense of unreality, of nightmarish fascination. How graceful he looked in slow motion, the dancer, his legs stretching as he leaped, his toes pointing, his arms outstretched.

"Have you ever seen such power in a jump? That ball was impossible! Rusty Rivers pulled this one out on sheer guts, start to finish! He's some kind of athlete. I've never seen anything like it."

"He's still on the ground in the end zone, John. We're waiting for a report . . . and here's the hit from a different angle. See how Rivers's head gets drilled into the artificial turf?"

She watched in dry-mouthed horror. Two bodies rammed into Rusty as he staggered across the goal line; one flew through the air with deadly grace, the other burst in from the ground. Then, he collapsed under their impact, landing curled protectively around the ball.

Throughout the replay the announcers kept up a running patter. How could they talk that way? How could they even think about the damned game, when Rusty was lying on the field not moving?

There was a soft ripple of applause, muffled through the glass window. Two men in white were pushing him off the field on a stretcher.

Rusty's voice echoed wildly in her mind. *I always land on my feet . . . on my feet . . . my feet . . .*

She had to get to him. She sprinted toward the door, felt the firm grasp of Gander's fingers on her wrist, and wrenched her arm away. "No!"

The wall phone rang, and Gander answered.

"Honey, it's the team doctor. Rusty wants you to meet him at Baylor Hospital." He hung up the phone. "Now, don't you worry your head over a thang," Gander Bodine drawled soothingly. "I'll get you to the hospital. We may even beat the ambulance."

Eleven

The double doors swung open with a whoosh, and it seemed that everyone in the E.R. waiting room snapped to attention, some even standing abruptly in anticipation.

A short, bespectacled man in charcoal slacks and a gold knit shirt stood in the doorway, scanning the anxious faces. He glanced down at the folder in his hands and frowned. "Kevyn Llewellyn?"

Kevyn hesitated, then forced herself to her feet and crossed the expanse of tiled floor. He offered his hand in brisk greeting.

"I'm Darrel Baughm, team doctor for the Gents. Rusty wanted me to tell you that he's doing fine. They just need to do a few tests."

"Doctor, you've told me what Rusty wanted me to hear. Now tell me the truth."

He did a double take, then nodded in agreement. "Okay, here's the way it is. He was out for several minutes, too long to take chances. He's still a little disoriented, but that's to be expected. Basically, the tests are just a precaution; we don't have any reason to believe he's sustained any serious damage, but with this kind of an injury there's always the possibility of neurological problems."

The words battered at her. How could this man be so calm, so casual, while he threw around words like that? This was *Rusty* he was talking about. She gripped the straps of her shoulder bag as if they could support her. Inhaling deeply, she fought to calm herself. "How long will it take?"

"I'm going up with him for the CAT scan, which ought to take thirty minutes, an hour,· maybe longer, depending on how they're staffed, today being a holiday. Why don't you just sit down, and I'll be back down as soon as I can."

"Do his parents know?"

"All that's being taken care of. You just take care of yourself. He's going to be all right."

The heavy doors swung open again, and an orderly reappeared with a football in his arms. Spotting Dr. Baughm, he hurried toward him, holding out the football. "Rivers is expecting a friend. He asked for you to give this to—"

With a wave of his hand, Baughm indicated Kevyn at his side. Gingerly, as if it were a lethal weapon, she accepted the football. Its rough texture was harsh against her palms, unwelcome and unyielding. And large, so much larger than she had realized.

"He asked for you to take care of it."

After they left, Kevyn sank onto the hard plastic chair. *Why me?* she wondered. She didn't want the football, couldn't stand the weight of it in her lap, in her heart. Curling her fingers around it, she explored its contours with the pads of her fingers, absorbing the feel of it. *His* fingers had grasped it, spanning its width and clutching it desperately, even as he was pounded into the turf. There was no residue of his warmth, nothing that identified it as his. But, he wanted it. He wanted her to keep it for him. And she would. Almost subconsciously, she cradled it to her breast and closed her eyes.

Rusty's a fighter. Memories washed over her. Oh, yes . . . he was definitely that. He fought when it was foolish to do so, yet sometimes he managed to wrest triumph from the certainty of failure, simply because it wasn't in him to quit. Her hands tightened their grip on the football.

The minutes dragged into an hour, and still no word. Fear clutched at her; she clutched the football in her arms. Desperately, she fought the panic welling up inside her.

"Ms. Llewellyn?"

Jerking to attention, she saw a young nurse in the doorway, holding the swinging door open and gesturing for her. Kevyn rushed to the nurse's side. "Please, is he all right?"

"Why don't you come in and see for yourself?" For the first time the young woman smiled. "We don't know anything yet. We're waiting for a doctor to read the CAT scan. It could be quite awhile."

CAT scan. Kevyn couldn't respond for the tightness in her throat, the constriction choking her breath away as the nurse led her down the corridor to the examining room where Rusty waited.

Kevyn's eyes were trained on the bed, on the man stretched out with his eyes squeezed shut, his neck braced in a cervical collar, one raised knee wrapped with a grotesque bulge of ice and bandage. "Rusty?" she whispered, fearful of waking him if he was resting.

Immediately, his head revolved toward her, and he greeted her with a weak smile. "Hello, beautiful."

"Hello, gorgeous," she responded softly, crossing to his side.

Then, his arm stretched out and his fingers tangled into her tousled mane of ebony hair, pulling her down to him. "You're a sight for sore eyes," he said in a raspy voice, and she felt his lips, hot and dry, on hers.

"How do you feel?" She drank in every detail of his appearance. His normally tanned features were pale, his eyes were hazed with pain.

"Like hell. I've gotta get out of here. I told them my head was fine. It's my knee I'm worried about." He pulled her even closer. "Help me get out of here, Kevyn. I've got to get back to Shreveport, to my dad. I don't care what any of these guys say. He's the best. He knows my knee better than anybody." But she saw the pain in his eyes as he lowered himself back to the pillow. "I think I'll just lay here and be

quiet awhile . . ." he murmured. He took her hand
in his and held it next to his roughened cheek.
"Thank the Lord, you're here, baby. Until you walked
in the room I thought all there was in the world was
sweat and antiseptic . . ." His eyes closed, and his
breathing steadied.

Kevyn felt pity, anger, relief. *I didn't want to love
you, Rusty Rivers. But, the Lord help me, I do.* A
lone tear trickled down her cheek and found the corner of her mouth. Tasting the saltiness, she brushed
it away with her free hand, wiping it on the football
by his side.

But, how much longer? How much longer could
she watch him do this to himself?

There was no answer.

An hour might have passed, maybe longer. But
finally the door opened and Dr. Baughm entered,
followed by a taller doctor, evidently the neurologist.

Rusty squinted at them, his grip on Kevyn's hand
tightening almost to the point of pain. "Well, what's
the verdict?"

Dr. Baughm spoke first. "Good news. The CAT
scan shows little active bleeding."

"Isn't that what I told you?" Rusty grumbled. "I've
had concussions before, you know. Hell, I've gone
back into a game with a concussion before."

Dr. Baughm, patted Rusty's shoulder agreeably.
"Well, we just had to be sure, didn't we?"

Rusty reached sulkily for his head and winced.
"But, this is just a concussion, right? That's what
you're telling me?"

"A relatively minor concussion," the other doctor
agreed reluctantly.

"Did they even bother to X-ray my knee, dammit?
Or talk to my dad? I'm gettin' out of here." He tried
to sit up, almost pulling Kevyn over on top of him
when he accidentally grabbed her arm instead of the
bed rail for leverage.

"Okay, Rusty," Dr. Baughm said. "Take it easy.
The Colonel's sending his private jet back for you,
so just settle down."

"Are you—are you sure it's safe to move him?" Kevyn asked.

Dr. Baughm nodded. "Rusty's right about one thing. He'll be better off in Shreveport, now that we know the extent of his cranial injury."

"And—and the bleeding. Is that—" She groped into the past for words, for terms that dredged up frightening, life-shattering memories. "Is that like a stroke? I mean, how do you *know* it won't rupture?"

The taller doctor's face reflected sudden compassion and understanding. "Mr. Rivers is suffering from a concussion, not a stroke. I take it you've had some experience with stroke?"

She swallowed hard. "My father."

"Then this must be very frightening to you. But I can assure you, Mr. Rivers's situation is not of that nature or severity."

Kevyn nodded mutely. Hadn't she heard such assurances before?

"Hey, Kev . . ." Rusty's face contorted with an attempted grin. "Don't worry about me. I'll be playing again in time for the Eagles. With any luck, I'll finish out the last three games of the season. Isn't that right, Doc?"

"Luck." It seemed that she could only speak in monosyllables, but the words fighting to pour from her lips were words she didn't dare speak.

Dr. Baughm patted Rusty's uninjured knee. "We'll sure do our damnedest. I'll go call the airport and see if the Colonel's plane has returned yet." Dr. Baughm excused himself, and the neurologist followed.

Choking back her tears, Kevyn took a shuddering breath. "Rusty, I'm scared. . . ."

"I shouldn't have brought you here," he muttered groggily. "I know this looks pretty awful, but I'm telling you, I'll be fine in a couple of days."

"Fine for what?" she whispered. "To go out and do it again?"

He didn't answer. He had drifted back asleep. And even if he hadn't, what answers did she expect?

She had to think. She had to get out, if even for a few moments. Overwhelmed by conflicting emotions, Kevyn stepped into the hallway. But once there, her distress only built as she stood alone in the bustling confusion of the E.R.

Dr. Baughm was at the nurses' desk using the telephone. She hurried to his side and waited for him to complete his call.

"We should be able to get Rusty out of here in about an hour," he said.

"Doctor, what Rusty said in there—about playing with a concussion. About being ready to play next week. He's not serious, is he?"

"As serious as he could be. It'll take more than a knock on the head to bench Rusty." The doctor patted a folder under his arm. "His knee X-rays have me worried, however. The sooner we can get him back to Shreveport, the better I'll feel. We need to get moving on that knee."

"It—it sounds like his knee's a higher priority than his head."

"Well, I'm certain if you asked Rusty, he'd tell you that it is."

Kevyn clenched her fists at her sides.

"Why don't you get a soft drink or some coffee? It'll be awhile before we leave, and you'll feel better. You can follow the signs to the snack machines."

"Yes," she said stiffly. "I think I'll do that."

The hallway of examining rooms stretched far in both directions. She turned blindly to the right and began walking. She needed a place to breathe, to think.

Kevyn, you're my inspiration. . . . I have to take this chance, this one chance, to make something of myself, and it starts right here. . . .

How could she keep on like this, pretending to understand what he was doing, helping to patch him up just so he could go back out and get hurt all over again? Automatic doors opened in front of her and she stepped through, finding herself in another long, cold hallway, but quiet, blessedly quiet. She leaned against the wall, fighting for composure. He wanted her to watch him destroy himself, and she couldn't do it. She just couldn't keep on doing it, dammit.

She had tried to preserve the barrier between them, to control how much she allowed his love to touch her, to believe that she could ignore what his game did to him, pretend the bruises came from an accidental fall, a clumsy mistake. A painful laugh tore from her throat. Rusty? Clumsy?

She started forward blindly. Damn him. *Damn him.* He had done this to her, had pushed her into accepting him, loving him, opening herself up to all the pain that she had known—*had known*—would follow their loving as surely as . . . surely as a headache would follow his damned concussion. He didn't mind the headaches, didn't mind the pain. But she did. She had tried to protect herself. Who else would if she didn't? She wanted to scream, to rage, but she couldn't scream her rage at him. He was hurt; that wouldn't be fair—

She rammed straight into a laundry cart. The blow knocked the wind out of her.

"Hey!" A man in hospital coveralls stopped the cart he was pushing. "Lady, this area's restricted to Environmental Services personnel."

She looked behind her, and couldn't remember even turning down this corridor. "I came from Emergency," she said.

He looked skeptical. "Lady, this is the laundry."

"How do I—how do I get back?"

"Your best bet from here is to go up to the main lobby and just follow the signs." He disappeared through the doorway nearest to her, one of several, and she couldn't read the signs and didn't know where any of the doors led or how far she'd come or—or—

She fought for air, for reason. A bank of elevators flanked the end of the hall. She approached them hesitantly. She could handle this. She'd handled situations like this all of her life. She raised her chin and was readying her excuses—she was blind as a bat without her glasses worked best—when the first elevator door opened and a flash of images registered: a gurney, people on either side of it, their faces knit with tension. They exploded from the elevator, tore past her—she pressed against the wall, her heart pounding. The empty elevator yawned threateningly at her. She didn't have any idea where it would take her, but feared instinctively it would be worse than the laundry room. The doors shuddered closed.

Biting her lower lip, she proceeded nervously past the elevators, turned yet another corner—how many corners had she turned? How would she ever find her way back?—and saw a gleaming escalator beckoning from the end of the corridor.

She picked up her pace and stepped onto it, grasping the rail like a lifeline. How long had she been gone? Was Rusty awake? How could she have left him alone?

She emerged in a large lobby, scanned it desperately for help, saw the gift shop, and remembered the kindly ladies who had operated the gift shop at the hospital when her father had died. She choked back a sob. She couldn't think about that now.

The gift shop smelled of potpourri; the front window displayed baskets of all sizes filled with scented dried petals, and Kevyn realized how desperately she had needed to cleanse herself of hospital smells and hospital memories. Several customers milled around, and a woman in a pink apron stood behind the counter, ringing up a sale. Kevyn looked past her to the telephone on the wall. *"Please,"* she said, and her tone of voice must have been less controlled than she realized, for she seemed to be drawing everyone's attention.

"May I help you?"

They were all staring, staring. . . . She forced herself to move to the counter. "I—I seem to have taken a wrong turn, and . . . I'm supposed to be in the Emergency Room."

The woman seemed considerably surprised. "This is the Roberts Building, but the Emergency Room is on the other side of—"

"I know. I mean, I know it's not anywhere around here. But—"

"We have a map outside in the lobby."

"I don't need a map," she said stiffly. Her hands were shaking. Why wouldn't they stop? She clenched them together, twining her fingers tightly. "I need someone who can show me the way."

"I'm sorry, ma'am."

"Could you—could you call the Emergency Room for me?"

"No, I'm sorry," the woman repeated. "But there are pay phones in the lobby."

Kevyn spun away and plunged back into the lobby. Terror assaulted her with an almost physical blow. She had to get back to Rusty. He had probably missed her, was worried about her, needed her—A running, squealing child bumped into her legs, and she couldn't even respond to the mother's apology. She dug in her purse even as she headed for the telephones. She plugged in a quarter and dialed information, requested the number for Baylor Emergency, concentrated *so hard*, and yet, somehow as she tried to punch the right buttons she got them wrong—couldn't remember the sequence—got a wrong number—called information again.

Rusty would be worried, distraught. He would be upset with her for leaving him when he needed her. . . . On the third try, she almost sobbed with relief when the number went through. She asked for Dr. Baughm.

"We have no one here by that—"

"You do. I mean, I know he's not on your staff, but he's with a patient, Rusty Rivers—or Sergei, I don't know how you have him listed."

"Please hold."

Hold. Hold on. Just hold on. Everything will be all right now. Guilt sucked all reason from her mind, left her almost quivering with fear.

She squeezed the receiver in her hand and fought to swallow, to ignore the voice that suddenly taunted her with a knowledge that sprang deep from a secret place inside of her—that it wasn't concern for Rusty that was driving her to panic, but fear for herself. She was the one who was lost, alone, desperate. Rusty was safety. He was security. He was strength.

She didn't want to be strong for him anymore. But she certainly wanted him to be strong for her. She fought down a lump of anger, of frustration, of confusion.

"Miss Llewellyn?" Dr Baughm's voice sounded very, very far away, as if it were at the other end of the world. "Miss Llewellyn? Nurse, are you sure this is the line—"

"I'm here," she said. "I . . . got hung up in the coffee shop." Was there a coffee shop? There had to be a coffee shop.

He laughed. "Well, I can put Rusty's fears at ease. He became quite agitated when he found out you weren't here."

"I'm sorry," she said. Guilt swept over her, and she was relieved. He needed her. She had to get back to him. "I shouldn't have left him alone. He's so worried about his knee."

"Actually, he seemed more worried about you. When I tried to show him his X rays, he insisted that I should go find you instead." He chuckled. "I think that blow to the head has him a little more disoriented than we realized."

"Really?" she asked, staring at graffiti scratched into the side of the phone booth, words she couldn't read. . . .

"Shall I tell him you'll be back soon?"

Shall I tell him you'll be scurrying back to safety, as soon as you find someone to take you by the hand and lead you like a helpless child? Shall I tell him you're quivering with fear in a phone booth in the same building—the same damned building—and you don't know which way to turn? Shall

I tell him you're only strong when you make the rules, otherwise you quit the game?

"Miss Llewellyn?"

"Tell Rusty—" She clenched her fists, fought down the lump of panic, groped for calm. "Tell Rusty that I have found another way back to Shreveport."

"But the Colonel's plane—"

She dug deep, deep, as she'd spent a lifetime doing, for excuses, subterfuges, and lies. "I ran into a friend. Someone I used as a model last year. She invited me to spend the night, and since there's nothing I can do for Rusty tonight anyway . . ."

"I see." She heard the cold disapproval in his voice but couldn't allow herself to care about his opinion.

She replaced the receiver and pressed her head against the wall of the booth. What next?

Slowly, she deposited another quarter, dialed *O*, and, waiting for the operator to answer, began rehearsing silently: *I'm in the most ridiculous situation. I'm in a phone booth and I dropped my contact lens in the dirt and I can't see to read the telephone directory and could you—*

Even as the operator answered, Kevyn hung up the phone.

Slowly, she crossed the lobby, back to the gift shop, back to the woman in pink, because she didn't know where else to go . . . and said the words that she had refused to ever speak again.

"Could you please help me get a taxi? I . . . I don't know how." She refused to take her eyes away from the woman's, no matter what she saw reflected there. "I can't read."

"Where the hell is she?" Rusty demanded, clenching the receiver.

"I don't know. I just don't know." Atticus's anxiety was evident in his voice. "I came to her apartment as soon as you called me. I haven't left all night."

"If you hear anything—"

"I'll call," Atticus responded forlornly for the fourth time that night.

Rusty hung up and buried his face in his hands. His head was about to split open. He'd discarded the damned cervical collar hours ago. And only the knowledge that the pain in his knee would be excruciating should he move kept him on the sectional with his leg elevated. He felt so helpless, so damned helpless. He stared out the window; outside, the lake was beginning to turn golden with the rising sun. Inside, the room was as black and dismal as his heart. Any light at all sent stabbing pain through his head. Every sound was amplified, from the shrill ringing of the telephone when his mother had called to scold him for not going to the hospital when he had arrived in Shreveport, to the occasional car or truck passing in front of his house.

And so, after hours of exhausting waiting, when yet another car seemed to pass, he was too lost in pain and fear to pay it any undue notice. When it slowed . . . he tensed. And when it drove off again, he fell back into a despair so deep that it was several moments before the slowly approaching footsteps registered in his pain-numbed, fear-frozen brain.

But when the doorbell rang, he lurched to his feet—to hell with the pain—and dragged himself toward the front door. By the time he got there, sweat was pouring from his body. His palm slipped off the doorknob the first time he tried to yank it open. But finally the door was open.

Kevyn stood there, washed in the first gray light of dawn, looking like hell and so damned beautiful it made tears sting his eyes. He slumped against the door frame. "Thank God . . ."

"And American Express," she responded shakily, stepping into his arms, which would be so warm, so right . . .

Only he put out his hand, using what little strength he had left to stop her short of embracing him. Within his weary heart, guilt and anger such as he'd never known in his life warred for prominence, and he couldn't cope with either. He saw in her eyes, in her outstretched arms, the yearning, the need, and could only shake his head. "No," he said. "I don't think so."

"Rusty, I'm so sorry."

"I know you are. So am I. But . . . I don't think I can handle that right now. Somebody—somebody's gotta call Atticus." And only when his knee was screaming with pain did he finally say, "I've got to sit down."

"What can I do?"

"Carry me?"

She slipped under his arm.

The effort of walking made further conversation impossible. Amidst much heaving and groaning, he finally got settled on the sofa. His head spun with a thousand questions, none of which seemed very significant now that she was here.

"I had you pegged from the start, didn't I?" she sobbed softly, kneeling in front of him to brush his hair out of his face. "More muscles than good sense."

"What every man needs," he said, "is a woman who understands him."

"Maybe this woman needs to try a little harder."

"This woman," he said, each word a struggle, "needs to promise not to move an inch . . . until I wake up."

"I promise," she whispered, and he felt the softness of her lips and the saltiness of her tears on his face, and finally, finally, succumbed to the exhaustion.

Kevyn sat cross-legged on the floor in front of him, a hot mug of clam chowder warming her hands. So intently was she watching him for any sign of distress, that she saw the first flutter of his eyelashes—those gorgeous eyelashes—when he began stirring. By the time his eyes opened, she'd risen to her knees and was hovering beside him.

"How do you feel?"

"Like hell."

"Do you want some soup? You can have cream of tomato, clam chowder, or cream of mushroom."

He rubbed his eyes. "I don't know. Whatever is open."

"They're all open." When he somehow managed to look askance and in devastating pain at the same time, Kevyn admitted nervously, "I was trying for chicken noodle, but . . . well, when you can't read the label, you make a few mistakes."

The sound that came from his lips was half-chuckle, half-moan. "Remind me not to let you choose the wine." He struggled until he was sitting fairly upright, with his leg still elevated. Only when he was settled did he really seem to see her. "Where'd you get that?"

She glanced down at the purple-and-yellow football jersey she was wearing, suddenly uneasy. "I found it in your drawer. It was the only thing I found that didn't swallow me completely." She placed the chowder in his hands and tilted it to his lips. Only when he had drained the mug by half did she finally speak, and even then, the words were difficult to find. "I want you to know, what happened yesterday . . . it'll never happen again."

"I know it won't." His expression was troubled, his voice so pained that suddenly she knew a fear that transcended anything she'd felt in Dallas.

She lowered the cup between them. What had she said the night before, when all she had wanted, had *needed*, was to feel his arms around her, to know that he loved her, that he was still wanting to help her—and he had warned her, warned her of what was surely happening now . . . when he told her how angry he was. She couldn't speak.

"Kevyn, I've had . . . I've had as much of this as I can take. This up and down, never knowing where I stand, always knowing that all it takes is one false move for everything to blow up in my face. I can't take it anymore, Kevyn. It's over. It's gotta be over."

He took her hand, and his was shaking. "It's all over."

"No." And she thought she had known pain before. . . . Kevyn rose slowly, shakily to her feet.

"It's too much to ask of anyone," he said. "I just can't live this way anymore, and I knew . . . I knew that you, of all people, would understand."

How could he be so calm? How could he throw everything away, without fighting, without—a sob choked in her throat.

"Kevyn, what's wrong? I thought—I thought you'd be relieved."

"You're telling me that it's all over between us, and I'm supposed to be relieved?"

"Between us? What are you talking about?" And as recognition dawned, he said, "Kevyn! I'm talking about football!"

"Football?" she echoed lamely. "You're saying that—that you're through with football?"

"I don't think I realized, until I saw your face yesterday, how crazy this business is. How unfair it is, how stupid it is to keep going when it's over, and you know it's over, and everybody else knows it's over—and how did you ever think I'd be able to let you go?" he asked, incredulous. "I couldn't do anything last night, just sit here in the dark and hurt and be afraid. And I promised myself that if I got through the night, I'd just go ahead with the surgery and retire and be done with it. Enough's enough."

"Surgery, what surgery?" she demanded.

"My dad saw the X rays. He says I have no choice but to undergo reconstructive surgery on my knee. At best, there's only a thirty percent chance that I'd ever be able to play again." He held out his arms to her. "It's over, baby. You don't have to watch it anymore. You don't have to hurt for me anymore. It's all over. We can get on with whatever it is we're going to do for the rest of our lives, and I'm hoping we'll be doing it together . . . won't we?"

And at last, at last, she felt his arms close around her, and knew safety and security and homecoming.

When she could finally move, finally speak again, she said, "Of course we'll be together. You're going to teach me to tell an *L* from a *T*—you notice," she said, choking on laughter and tears, "that I didn't say you're going to teach me to read. I don't know if I'll ever be able to, but I'm willing to try, one step at a time, as long as you're there with me."

"You know I will be." He crushed her against him, and she was flooded with joy. "You know it."

"And—and if you think I'm going to let you give up with thirty-seventy odds, you're a crazier jock than I thought. Do you know what the payoff at Louisiana Downs is on those kinds of odds?" she demanded.

"What are you talking about?"

"Your knee, Rusty. You're talking with your head, not your heart. Your head says it's time to quit. What does your heart say?"

"I—I don't know. I hurt too much and in too many places to be sure."

"Then I'll tell you. I'll tell you exactly what I think about you and your football, and your had-it-all-too-easy charmed life. When I was stuck at the airport for seven hours, when I saw two planes to Shreveport fill up with Gents fans on their way home after the game and heard them talking—about you, Rusty, about you—I was so proud. Because they saw what I know—that you've got heart, a heart as big as the sky. That no matter what people have said about you, no matter how many nosedives your career took, you were still in there fighting, and you refused to quit, and—and—" She was so filled with emotion, with desperation to make him understand, that suddenly words seemed inadequate. She took his rough cheeks between her palms, held his face, stared straight into his beautiful eyes, and said, "Rusty, don't quit yet. Please, just for me, tell me that *today* you haven't quit. Maybe tomorrow. Maybe after the surgery, when you know more. Maybe if your knee doesn't mend right—"

"How can you say that," he asked huskily. "My dad's the best there is."

"Maybe, when you look in the mirror and can look yourself in the face and say, 'I'm ready for it to end.' But not today. That's all I ask. Please, not today."

"And what if . . . what if that means this happens to me again?" he asked quietly. "Or worse? How can I put you through this again? I still don't know how you got back here, but I could think of a thousand disasters and you helpless in the middle of all of them—and believe me, I didn't believe that old-friend story for one minute."

"I have a confession to make, Rusty."

"I'm listening."

"Last night, I put you through hell. I know that, and I feel so guilty, but . . . last night was one of the best nights of my entire life."

"I think you'd better explain."

"I was terrified. I didn't know what to do. I didn't have enough money for the taxi, but the cab driver was so nice. I know he must have thought I was an idiot, but he *did* want his money, so he showed me how to get cash with my credit card. And then, when I had to buy my ticket to Shreveport . . . I was so afraid. I had to sign to charge it, and—and I told you, I have trouble with my *L*'s—and the man looked at it, and the expression on his face—I thought I would die." She felt her cheeks flaming, and plunged forward. "And he asked to see my driver's license, and I showed it to him, and he didn't say another word. He didn't even question me. He seemed a little curious, that's all. Rusty, nobody cared. Even when I had to ask for help, and even when I had to say 'I don't know how' and 'I can't read the instructions,' they were so nice, so nice." She didn't realize she was crying, until he wiped her cheeks with his large, rough hands. "They weren't laughing. They weren't cruel."

"Kevyn," he said gently. "I've been booed by over 50,000 people when I dropped a pass, but I've never known anything that hurt as much as being an eight-year-old 'ballerina boy.' Why do you think that to this day I don't like having reporters hound me about my dancing, and sportscasters and comedians making jokes about it? Not because I'm ashamed of it, but because some hurts stay too close to the surface." He traced her cheekbone with his index finger, trailed a path to her lips, then kissed them. "But you're not dealing with kids who don't know any better now. And now you can tell the difference."

"You know what I keep remembering?" she asked quietly, her eyes roaming every contour of his face, every line, every shadow. "I owe you a half a mile."

"What are you saying?" A muscle jerked in his tensed jaw, betraying the force he was using to constrain his emotions.

"I'm saying I stopped you from competing once before—I thought I was doing what was right." She ran her tongue nervously over her lips, then raised her eyes to his. "I won't stand in your way, ever again." Tossing her hair out of her face, she raised her trembling chin defiantly. "I owe you a half a mile, and I fully intend to repay that debt, if I have to carry you across the finish line."

"Kevyn, that race was nothing compared to what I have in front of me." His eyes met hers, uncertain, unsure. "What if I get traded?"

"We'll move."

"And if I get hurt?"

"We'll manage."

"And if—"

"I know all that, Rusty. We're worth fighting for, aren't we?" And then his arms were around her, his lips were capturing hers. For a moment, just a moment, she thought she heard the roar of the crowd and tasted triumph on his lips, and she knew that no matter what happened . . .

They'd already won the big one.

EPILOGUE

Associated Press

Shreveport, La.—Ending an eleven-year career,

Confederate Gents wide receiver Rusty Rivers announced his retirement from professional football at a news conference today.

Rivers played for the Washington Redskins, where he was a member of their first Super Bowl Championship team, then was traded to the Buffalo Bills and Phoenix Cardinals, for whom he played one season each. At a point when his career seemed ended, he was picked up by the then-new Shreveport Gents. He spent the last six years of his career as a starter for that team, representing them in four Pro Bowls, and was voted All-Pro his final season. Rivers will continue to reside in Shreveport, his hometown, with his wife, artist Kevyn Llewellyn, and their two children.

THE EDITOR'S CORNER

In publishing a series such as LOVESWEPT we couldn't function without timetables, schedules, deadlines. It seems we're always working toward one, only to reach it then strive for another. I mention the topic because many of you write and ask us questions about the way we work and about how and when certain books are published. Just consider this Editor's Corner as an example. I'm writing this in early April, previewing our October books, which will run in our September books, which will be on sale in August. The books you're reading about were scheduled for publication at least nine months earlier and were probably written more than a year before they reach your hands! Six books a month means seventy-two a year, and we're into our seventh year of publication. That's a lot of books and a lot of information to try to keep up with. Amazingly, we do keep up—and so do our authors. We enjoy providing you with the answer to a question about a particular book or author or character. Your letters mean a lot to us.

In our ongoing effort to extend the person-to-person philosophy of LOVESWEPT, we are setting up a 900 number through which you can learn what's new—and what's old—with your favorite authors! Next month's Editor's Corner will have the full details for you.

Kay Hooper's most successful series for us to date has been her *Once Upon a Time . . .* novels. These modern-day fairy tales have struck a chord with you, the readers, and your enjoyment of the books has delighted and inspired Kay. Her next in this series is LOVESWEPT #426, **THE LADY AND THE LION,** and it's one of Kay's sizzlers. Keith Donovan and Erin Prentice first speak to each other from their adjacent hotel balconies, sharing secrets and desperate murmurings in the dark. Kay creates a moody, evocative, emotionally charged atmosphere in which these two kindred spirits fall in love before they ever meet. But when they finally do set eyes on each other, they know without having to speak that they've found their destinies. This wonderful story will bring out the true romantic in all of you!

We take you from fairy tales to fairyland this month! Our next LOVESWEPT, #427, **SATIN SHEETS AND STRAWBERRIES** by Marcia Evanick, features a golden-haired nymph of a heroine named Kelli SantaFe. Hero Logan Sinclair does a double take when he arrives at what looks like Snow White's cottage in search of his aunt and uncle—and finds a bewitching woman dressed as a fairy. Kelli runs her business from her home and at first resents Logan's interference and the tug-of-war he wages for his relatives, whom she'd taken in and treated like the family

(continued)

she'd always wanted. Logan is infuriated by her stubbornness, yet intrigued by the woman who makes him feel as though his feet barely touch the ground. Kelli falls hard for Logan, who can laugh at himself and rescue damsels in distress, but who has the power to shatter her happiness. You'll find you're enchanted by the time Kelli and Logan discover how to weave their dreams together!

All of us feel proud and excited whenever we publish a new author in the line. The lady whose work we're introducing you to next month is a talented, hardworking mother of five who strongly believes in the importance of sprinkling each day with a little romance. We think Olivia Rupprecht does just that with **BAD BOY OF NEW ORLEANS**, LOVESWEPT #428. I don't know about you, but some of my all-time favorite romances involve characters who reunite after years apart. I find these stories often epitomize the meaning of true love. Well, in **BAD BOY OF NEW ORLEANS** Olivia reunites two people whose maddening hunger for each other has only deepened with time. Hero Chance Renault can still make Micah Sinclair tremble, can still make her burn for his touch and cry out for the man who had loved her first. But over time they've both changed, and a lot stands between them. Micah feels she must prove she can survive on her own, while Chance insists she belongs to him body and soul. Their journey toward happiness together is one you won't want to miss!

Joan Elliott Pickart never ceases to amaze me with the way she is able to provide us with winning romance after winning romance. She's truly a phenomenon, and we're pleased and honored to bring you her next LOVESWEPT, #429, **STORMING THE CASTLE**. While reunited lovers have their own sets of problems to overcome, when two very different people find themselves falling in love, their long-held beliefs, values, and lifestyles become an issue. In **STORMING THE CASTLE,** Dr. Maggie O'Leary finds her new hunk of a neighbor, James-Steven Payton, to be a free spirit, elusive as the wind and just as irresistible. Leave it to him to choose the unconventional over the customary way of doing things. But Maggie grew up with a father who was much the same, whose devil-may-care ways often brought heartache. James-Steven longs to see the carefree side of Maggie, and he sets out to get her to smell the flowers and to build sand castles without worrying that the tide will wash them away. Though Maggie longs to join her heart to his, she knows they must first find a common ground. Joan handles this tender story beautifully. It's a real heart-warmer!

One author who always delivers a fresh, innovative story is Mary Kay McComas. Each of her LOVESWEPTs is unique and imaginative—never the same old thing! In **FAVORS**, LOVESWEPT #430, Mary Kay has once again let her creative juices flow, and
(continued)

the result is a story unlike any other. Drawing on her strength in developing characters you come to know intimately and completely, Mary Kay serves up a romance filled with emotion and chock full of fun. Her tongue-in-cheek portrayal of several secondary characters will have you giggling, and her surprise ending will add the finishing touch to your enjoyment of the story. When agent Ian Walker is asked to protect a witness as a favor to his boss, he considers the job no more appealing than baby-sitting—until he meets Trudy Babbitt, alias Pollyanna. The woman infuriates him by refusing to believe she's in danger—and ignites feelings in him he'd thought were long dead. Trudy sees beneath Ian's crusty exterior and knows she can transform him with her love. But first they have to deal with the reality of their situation. I don't want to give away too much, so I'll just suggest you keep in mind while reading **FAVORS** that nothing is exactly as it seems. Crafty Mary Kay pulls a few aces from her sleeve!

One of your favorite authors—and ours—Billie Green returns to our lineup next month with **SWEET AND WILDE**, #431. Billie has always been able to capture that indefinable quality that makes a LOVESWEPT romance special. In her latest for us, she throws together an unlikely pair of lovers, privileged Alyson Wilde and streetwise Sid Sweet and sends them on an incredible adventure. You might wonder what a blue-blooded lady could have in common with a bail bondsman and pawnshop owner, but Billie manages to keep her characters more than a little bit interested in each other. When thirteen-year-old Lenny, who is Alyson's ward, insists that his friend Sid Sweet is a great guy and role model, Alyson decides she has to meet the tough-talking man for herself. And cynical Sid worries that Good Samaritan Alyson has taken Lenny on only as her latest "project." With Lenny's best interests at heart, they go with him in search of his past and end up discovering their own remarkable future— one filled with a real love that is better than any of their fantasies.

Be sure to pick up all six books next month. They're all keepers!
Sincerely,

Susann Brailey

Susann Brailey
Editor
LOVESWEPT
Bantam Books
666 Fifth Avenue
New York, NY 10103

FAN OF THE MONTH

Sandra Beattie

How did I come to be such a fan of LOVESWEPT romances? It was by accident, really. My husband was in the Australian Navy and we were moving once again to another state. I wanted some books to read while we stayed in the motel, so I went to a second-hand bookstore in search of some Silhouette romances. I spotted some books I hadn't seen before, and after reading the back covers I decided to buy two. I asked the saleslady to set the rest aside in case I wanted them later. I read both books that night and was hooked. I raced back to the store the next day and bought the rest. I've been a fan of LOVESWEPT ever since.

My favorite authors are Sandra Brown, Kay Hooper, Iris Johansen, Fayrene Preston, Joan Elliott Pickart, and Mary Kay McComas. The thing I like about LOVESWEPT heroes is that they are not always rich and handsome men, but some are struggling like us. I cry and laugh with the people in the books. Sometimes I become them and feel everything that they feel. The love scenes are just so romantic that they take my breath away. But then some of them are funny as well.

I'm thirty-four years old, the mother of three children. I love rock and roll, watching old movies, and snuggling up to my husband on cold, rainy nights. If there is one thing I can pass on to other readers, it is that you can't let everything get you down. When I feel depressed, I pick up a LOVESWEPT and curl up in a chair for a while and just forget about everything. Then when I get up again, the world doesn't look so bad anymore. Try it, it really works!

OFFICIAL RULES TO
LOVESWEPT'S
DREAM MAKER GIVEAWAY
(See entry card in center of this book)

1. NO PURCHASE NECESSARY. To enter both the sweepstakes and accept the risk-free trial offer, follow the directions published on the insert card in this book. Return your entry on the reply card provided. If you do not wish to take advantage of the risk-free trial offer, but wish to enter the sweepstakes, return the entry card only with the "FREE ENTRY" sticker attached, or send your name and address on a 3x5 card to : Loveswept Sweepstakes, Bantam Books, PO Box 985, Hicksville, NY 11802-9827.

2. To be eligible for the prizes offered, your entry must be received by September 17, 1990. We are not responsible for late, lost or misdirected mail. Winners will be selected on or about October 16, 1990 in a random drawing under the supervision of Marden Kane, Inc., an independent judging organization, and except for those prizes which will be awarded to the first 50 entrants, prizes will be awarded after that date. By entering this sweepstakes, each entrant accepts and agrees to be bound by these rules and the decision of the judges which shall be final and binding. This sweepstakes will be presented in conjunction with various book offers sponsored by Bantam Books under the following titles: Agatha Christie "Mystery Showcase", Louis L'Amour "Great American Getaway", Loveswept "Dreams Can Come True" and Loveswept "Dream Makers". Although the prize options and graphics of this Bantam Books sweepstakes will vary in each of these book offers, the value of each prize level will be approximately the same and prize winners will have the options of selecting any prize offered within the prize level won.

3. Prizes in the Loveswept "Dream Maker" sweepstakes: Grand Prize (1) 14 Day trip to either Hawaii, Europe or the Caribbean. Trip includes round trip air transportation from any major airport in the US and hotel accomodations (approximate retail value $6,000); Bonus Prize (1) $1,000 cash in addition to the trip; Second Prize (1) 27" Color TV (approximate retail value $900).

4. This sweepstakes is open to residents of the US, and Canada (excluding the province of Quebec), who are 18 years of age or older. Employees of Bantam Books, Bantam Doubleday Dell Publishing Group Inc., their affiliates and subsidiaries, Marden Kane Inc. and all other agencies and persons connected with conducting this sweepstakes and their immediate family members are not eligible to enter this sweepstakes. This offer is subject to all applicable laws and regulations and is void in the province of Quebec and wherever prohibited or restricted by law. In order to win a prize, residents of Canada will be required to correctly answer a time-limited arithmetical skill-testing question.

5. Winners will be notified by mail and will be required to execute an affidavit of eligibility and release which must be returned within 14 days of notification or an alternate winner will be selected. Prizes are not transferable. Trip prize must be taken within one year of notification and is subject to airline departure schedules and ticket and accommodation availability. Winner must have a valid passport. No substitution will be made for any prize except as offered. If a prize should be unavailable at sweepstakes end, sponsor reserves the right to substitute a prize of equal or greater value. Winners agree that the sponsor, its affiliates, and their agencies and employees shall not be liable for injury, loss or damage of any kind resulting from an entrant's participation in this offer or from the acceptance or use of the prizes awarded. Odds of winning are dependant upon the number of entries received. Taxes, if any, are the sole responsibility of the winners. Winner's entry and acceptance of any prize offered constitutes permission to use the winner's name, photograph or other likeness for purposes of advertising and promotion on behalf of Bantam Books and Bantam Doubleday Dell Publishing Group Inc. without additional compensation to the winner.

6. For a list of winners (available after 10/16/90), send a self addressed stamped envelope to Bantam Books Winners List, PO Box 704, Sayreville, NJ 08871.

7. The free gifts are available only to entrants who also agree to sample the Loveswept subscription program on the terms described. The sweepstakes prizes offered by affixing the "Free Entry" sticker to the Entry Form are available to all entrants, whether or not an entrant chooses to affix the "Free Books" sticker to the Entry Form.